# Cotswold Mistress

# COTSWOLD MISTRESS

## Michael Spicer

St. Martin's Press
New York

Library of Congress Cataloging-in-Publication Data

Spicer, Michael.
   Cotswold mistress / Michael Spicer.
      p.    cm.
   "A Thomas Dunne book."
   ISBN 0-312-07683-5
   I. Title.
   PR6069.P498C628   1992
   823'.914-dc20
                                                    92-3020
                                                    CIP

First published in Great Britain by Constable & Company Limited.

First U.S. Edition: June 1992
10 9 8 7 6 5 4 3 2 1

To Thea, my mother-in-law


Needless to say, all the characters in this book are totally fictitious and are not meant to bear a direct resemblance to any living person. The events also are entirely fictional. What is historically true is that at least twenty-two scientists and engineers working on British defence projects died prematurely between 1982 and 1988.

# 1

'I want to shift you from counter-terrorism to anti-espionage,' the chief had declared.

'Is that promotion?' I had asked.

He had smiled and said, 'Don't be awkward, Jane. Anti-espionage may have become unfashionable since the so-called end of the cold war, but you and I know we still need it as much, indeed, as we continue to need counter-subversion. There may be an army coup in what was the Soviet Union any day now. That would make our political masters think twice about changing our role. Even if the Russians have decided to lie low for the time being, the same, unfortunately, cannot be said of our Arabian brethren.'

And that had been the end of the interview.

It had occurred to me, as I got up to leave, that the chief had not seemed entirely convinced himself by what he had just said. It was distinctly possible that he was merely being the good civil servant practising the art of protecting his patch from what were, for him, new and unfamiliar predators. Was it not true – in a way that would have been unthinkable a few years earlier – that the Public Accounts Committee of Parliament had begun to make some attempts to take a friendly interest in his budgets? And, what was worse, that the Treasury had actually managed to do so? So was it possible that I had been a witness to the astonishing phenomenon of the head of Britain's counter intelligence services working up publicly presentable arguments as to why his job should continue to exist and, what's more, doing so in front of one of his own agents?

I stared down at the Atlantic surf crashing on to the white, hot sand twenty feet below. The television weather woman had forecast a gale-force wind building up in the Caribbean to the south and east. It would probably turn into a hurricane by the time it hit the Florida coast. These winds, I knew, had a habit of gathering force as they left the islands and headed for the North American mainland. Already the waves were beginning to coil in anticipation, and streaks of toothpaste like foam crisscrossed the otherwise deep-blue ocean. Behind me the elegant Edwardian facade of the Breakers Hotel, flagship of West Palm Beach, seemed to be bracing itself for the lashing it might reasonably expect to receive within the next few hours.

I loosened the collar of my white cotton shirt. The sun blazed down on me; the humidity was beginning to make me sweat. Even with these distractions, I found it impossible for the moment to take my mind off my boss back home. I imagined the anonymous office in the centre of London, where no doubt even now he would be lounging in one corner of his sofa, his long elegant legs stretched out at an angle along the edge of the seat. If he was in a 'one-to-one' meeting, his guest would be sunk awkwardly beside him in a large wing chair. This had apparently been systematically stuffed with soft spongey cushioning that placed its occupant at a calculated disadvantage. As the base of his spine was sucked deeper into the recesses of the chair, so the arguments of any protagonist would go down with it.

I suppose it was the chief's capacity to surprise that I found especially attractive. Without being in any way mercurial, he had an enormous repertoire of moods, often tailoring each one to meet a particular need: one moment effusively polite, the next reflective, then all of a sudden brutally – and, it has to be said, sometimes hurtfully – pointed and aggressive. What made all this rather sexy was that it appeared to be done with such self-control. He was one of the very few men whom I had known over a reasonable period of time, and who had apparently found me quite agreeable, who had not made so much as a hint of a pass at me. His deep blue eyes often smiled but they never flirted. Nor, I suspect, was there anything unusual about the treatment I received. The chief did not appear to have favourites.

I lifted my gaze to the horizon, where an ominous mountain of clouds was forming. I wondered what plans he would have for me on my return. I assumed that there must have been some positive reasons for having moved me off the work with the Irish Republican Army. I certainly found it hard to believe that there could have been any serious dissatisfaction with what I had been doing in that field. It was generally known, at least by the top brass, that I had made one or two useful breakthroughs in recent months. Personally, I was rather sorry that I was not to be allowed to exploit these gains. What is more, I suspected that this sadness at my departure from the Irish task force would not be shared by several senior members of the Republican Army. They had begun to make it clear that they had become less than overjoyed by my growing involvement in their affairs, so much so that they had recently taken the trouble to destroy my car with a pad of Semtex, but strangely enough without my being inside it.

I was once again on the point of going through in my mind the alternative explanations of why the IRA had allowed me to escape in this way, when my thoughts were suddenly interrupted by the slamming of a porch door immediately behind me.

A voice shouted, 'My God, this wind has come up from nowhere. It was hardly a breeze half an hour ago.' I turned round and pressed my bottom against the sea wall.

'It's going to be quite a storm,' I said.

Simon Carey stumbled toward me, his fair, boyish hair blowing out of control. Despite having known him for most of my life (we had grown up together from the time we were teenagers), I was still capable of being surprised by his startlingly good looks. If anything, these had improved with age. His pink, soft, adolescent skin had in his twenties become tanned and taut. In recent years it had turned hard and leathery and very masculine. The firm eyebrows, well-cut straight nose, and rounded, often smiling lips each made its contribution to his strong, squarely symmetrical face. Nor was his appearance deceptive. As a veteran of the Falklands war and, now, in his midthirties, as aide to the governor of Hong Kong, his qualities had been recognized by others. It has to be said that his future had not always been imagined as rosy. In his younger days he had spent so much of his time playing sports for the army that his superior officers had begun to overlook his military ambitions. In order to put this right, he had had virtually to give up playing both rugby and cricket and to concentrate on being a professional soldier.

He was breathing deeply as he came up close to me.

'You're getting out of shape,' I teased.

Ignoring this, he said, 'Jane, darling, they're here. They must have been in the lobby for quite a while. Apparently they've been trying to call us in our room. I've been out looking for an English newspaper. Breakers seem to have sold out of them. I've been told they sell yesterday's *Financial Times* two blocks down the street, but I haven't had time to get there.'

'Let them wait one minute longer,' I said, and I put my right arm inside his blue-and-white-striped linen jacket, which since arriving in America he wore in place of his regimental blazer. I pressed the tips of my fingers against the small of his back. He lifted me into his arms and swung me several feet into the air. Our kiss was much more than the release of lust. I had begun to love him and the feeling seemed to be mutual.

When he placed me on the ground, he said, 'We really had better be going. You know what Marvin's like. Not a man to be kept waiting for too long. What's more, he's brought Lucille. Apparently he wants to take us out to lunch.'

'Wouldn't it be wiser to stay in the hotel with this storm brewing up? Breakers looks pretty solidly built. I think I'd rather be in there than be blown from one street cafe to another.'

'Not so silly as it sounds,' he said. 'I've just heard someone say as I was coming out that the forecasters have upgraded the storm to severe hurricane; that can be quite nasty.'

'I know. I was in one once in South America.

Two people beside me were killed by falling masonry.'

'I gather Marvin's brought his limousine and his chauffeur. So at least we won't get wet and we'll ask him to take us to a restaurant made of solid concrete so we won't blow away. What more could we ask for?'

'Edible food,' I said. 'I'm starving.'

'Knowing Marvin, we'll probably get that, too.'

I suddenly had a yearning to have Simon to myself.

'Do we really have to go out to lunch?' I asked. 'I'd much rather be alone with you.'

'Very flattering,' he said, 'but we can't let him down now. And, as I say, he's got Lucille with him.'

I pulled a face, but allowed him to drag me by my hand toward the back entrance of the hotel. If there had been a real choice between room service (followed by more love making) and rubbing knees in an expensive downtown eating establishment with Marvin and his bosom-heaving, diamond-dripping girlfriend, I knew which I would have gone for. The fact was that we were committed to Marvin, and I knew it. Once inside the hotel building, Simon had some difficulty in closing the door to the beach. At last he was able to secure the latch and we were suddenly insulated from the howl of the rising wind. In the relative quiet of a small entrance lobby, I was able to drop my voice.

'Let's at least stop Marvin boasting about his female conquests. I'm sure he only does it to annoy Lucille. The trouble is that he succeeds. Every time he talks about another woman, the top half of her body almost pops out on to her plate in fury. It's very alarming.'

Simon laughed. 'Marvin's only interest at the moment seems to be his Learjet. He gave me an earful about it just now. Apparently he's only managed to hangar it for one night. It seems that every other person in Florida wants to house an aeroplane for the next few days. I know that if I owned one, I'd use it to fly as far away from this place as possible. The idea of squabbling over the privilege of keeping it on the ground around here, however well protected, seems bizarre to me.'

'They're used to hurricanes in Florida,' I said.

'I doubt if they're used to anything like the one that's going to hit us in the next few hours.'

# 2

I slipped the gear-stick of my Mercedes sports-car into overdrive and contemplated an unusually straight stretch of Cotswold Road. It was a warm late summer evening and I had pulled back the sunroof to allow the country air to blow through my hair.

The holiday in Florida had become a fading memory. It had all been a year ago now. The eye of the hurricane had changed course at the last moment and had landed in South Carolina, killing five people and injuring many more. A few days later, Simon had returned to his job in Hong Kong. I had gone back to a London office building with an underground parking lot, shuttered and barred ground-floor windows, and a roof bristling with communications antennae. From here I had spent the last twelve months monitoring the movements of various ladies and gentlemen from what used to be called the Soviet Union. No one seemed to have informed them (or me) that we had won the cold war or that their country had disintegrated. They persisted in paying people to demonstrate and, if possible, riot in our streets, and in stealing industrial secrets.

The better looking of them attempted to seduce the randier members of our armed forces. I assumed our people were still doing much the same thing in their territories.

To be perfectly honest, I found this work faintly ridiculous, almost childish, given the changes on the world scene. I didn't even need the money they paid me. The legacy left to me by my late ex-husband, Lord John Hildreth, was enough to cover even my extravagant life-style.

The chief appeared quite unmoved by my irritation, which he must have detected or have had reported back to him. On the occasions I had bumped into him, he seemed to be singularly unmoved by anything at all. His lean, angular face beamed good cheer when he passed me in the corridor, and his eyes – which could at times be anything but joyous – appeared to have taken on a permanent twinkle of merriment.

He came close at one point to giving himself away.

'Boyfriend okay?' he asked one day.

The fact that he knew about Simon was hardly surprising. I knew he received regular updates of all our personal and confidential files. (I would have given good money to have had a look at the chief's own private file. No one – not at least anyone I spoke to – knew even whether he was married.) I supposed he had formed a view about the cause of my low spirits. Presumably he had been informed that I thought I was in love with Simon, perhaps even that I *was* in love with him. I had seen Simon only twice in the past twelve months, when he had made fleeting official visits to London on behalf of the Hong Kong government. The chief had no doubt assessed the effect of this on my morale, and thus on my usefulness to the service. This in turn, I imagine, explained why he kept me on the Russian Embassy patrol.

Ahead of me the road rolled across the hills toward Stow-on-the-Wold. In the valley behind me, just out of view of my mirror, lay Burford, with its bow-fronted tea shops, its ironmongers, delicatessens, gray-stone pubs and, it has to be said, its multitude of fat-bottomed tourists in splitting-tight shorts. I looked at my watch: just after seven. Not for the first time, I considered changing my mind and giving Marvin Lockhart's party a miss. Accepting his invitation seemed increasingly like an act of treachery against Simon. This feeling had strengthened over the last few days, the more certain I had become that Marvin had come over without the flamboyant Lucille Fraser. There had certainly been no mention of her in the letter of invitation he had sent me two weeks previously.

The light outside was beginning to fade fast now. A group of poplar trees on a distant ridge had become a line of black silhouettes waving against a sky that was turning gray-blue. I leaned forward and switched on my headlights.

The harvest was almost fully gathered, and fields of luminous yellow stubble reflected back at a pale premature moon. Across the landscape, smoking black scars marked the places where the leftovers of the corn had been burnt to save the farmers the cost of ploughing the stalks back into the ground.

Marvin's invitation had been strangely formal. Typed on Claridge's writing paper, it had been delivered by hand to my house in Montpellier Square. Its heavy black letters had stuck out almost threateningly from the crisp hotel notepaper. The words themselves had announced that Mr Marvin Lockhart had rented

Giddlington Manor for the duration of the pheasant-shooting season and that he would much like to renew the acquaintance of Lady Jane Hildreth at a small cocktail party he was giving for a few friends at the manor on Friday the tenth of September. There was no mention of Simon Carey, nor of Lucille Fraser.

I now had the perfect excuse for skipping the party. The traffic coming out of London on the M40 had been appalling. The invitation was for drinks and I could truthfully say that by the time I had circled around Oxford it had been too late to return to my cottage in Chipping Campden, change, and drive the fifteen miles or so to reach Marvin's house before the rest of his guests would have left.

At the back of my mind was the thought that my arrival without Simon might send Marvin the wrong signals. He was a very rich man used to getting his own way, especially where women were concerned. The blowsy, easy-going, and physically seductive Lucille had seemed to me to be ideally cast for this assignment. I was not, especially in my present mood.

I reached the T-junction at the A429 and turned right for Stow-on-the-Wold. Within a minute I would have to make the decision whether to go left for the Slaughters and Little Giddlington, or to continue straight on for Chipping Campden and home.

I had to admit there was no need to change my clothes. I was wearing a smart blue suit that I had recently bought from Belville Sassoon. It would certainly do for an early-evening cocktail party. I was fortunate that my long blond hair never needed more than a few strokes of a brush to make it presentable. With a spray of Ma Griffe behind the ears, attendance at Marvin Lockhart's party was definitely an option, one I chose to exercise for the same reason that I had left London early in the first place. I might well have ignored his letter. It was the telephone call following it that had really intrigued me.

There had been a strange urgency in Marvin's voice when he had said, almost pleadingly, 'It's been such a long time, Jane. I do hope you will be able to make it on Friday. I may need your help – professionally, I mean.' As far as I could recollect, we had never discussed my profession.

Once I had turned off the A429, the road became narrow and winding. Smoke was curling from the chimneys of the honey-coloured Cotswold cottages dotted at intervals along the route. I drove for about ten minutes along this road, until I came to a low stone wall, which ran continuously for about half a mile on the right. I knew from the directions I had been sent that this marked the boundary of the estate that Marvin had rented. The entrance to the grounds was indicated by a large stone archway that rose up in front of me, just before the wall turned northward around a sharp right-hand corner. Once I was under the arch, the view ahead of me, even in the falling dusk, was breathtaking. I was facing down a perfectly straight Tarmac driveway that stretched ahead almost as far as the eye could see. An avenue of dark blue conifers, some hundred feet high, was interspersed with smaller maples. It was hard to make out their colours in the dimming light, but they appeared to have yellow-green leaves that contrasted with the darkness of the giant conifers. Immaculately cut lawns sloped gently down from the base of the trees to the edge of the road. In the far distance, possibly a mile away, what I took to be the house itself was a blur of grey and blue. The whole effect was of a combination of grandeur and harmony more typical, I suppose, of French neoclassical landscaping than of a British garden.

I drove slowly for several minutes, contemplating what I would find when I reached the house. Away to my left a lake, which I had not noticed before, rippled from behind the trees. It occurred to me how little I really knew of Marvin Lockhart. Simon and I had first met him and Lucille at a dinner party in Florida given for us by a distant relative of Simon's. Almost from the start of the evening, they had pressed invitations on us to visit Marvin's three Florida houses. Eventually we had succumbed and had subsequently been taken on several conducted tours around his libraries, wine cellars, gardens, swimming pools, boats, and cars, not to mention the Learjet.

Marvin came from a banking family, which had apparently made its fortune lending money around Florida, especially to the Ringling circus people, although he himself claimed to be more interested in books than in money lending.

It was not, however, for his literary knowledge that Mr Lockhart was known around the state of Florida, nor, for that matter for his wealth, nor even for his taste in women. His gambling, womanizing, and book collecting paled into insignificance when compared with his real obsession. What really made Marvin get up and brush his teeth in the morning was a total fascination with warplanes. He was, in fact, an amateur designer, engineer, and inventor of military aircraft. Not that any of his creations had so far actually gone into production, but there were apparently several of his prototypes dotted around various airfields across the United States. Nothing came even close to rivalling them for his interest and

19

attention. They were no doubt his real consolation for never having found himself a wife.

Knowing at least this much about him, I thought it most peculiar that he should have decided to rent the vast establishment I was now approaching. The closer I got to the building, the stranger the whole thing appeared. It really was an extraordinary place for one man to set himself up in, for however short a period of time, and Marvin had indicated that he planned to stay there at least until Christmas.

I can only describe the house that rose up in front of me as a mini-Blenheim Palace. Like the majestic home that the victorious Duke of Marlborough had built for himself, its Georgian frontage spanned two symmetrical square wings that jutted out at the front. It was built, surprisingly, not of Cotswold stone, but in a greyer variety that one finds, for instance, in the Mendips in Somerset. About a dozen steps led up from the drive, under a balcony, to a polished oak double door. The scale of the building reminded me a little of Greysham Park, where I had lived for the three years of my marriage.

I parked my Mercedes amongst an assortment of private cars on a patch of gravel to the left of the steps. I reached for the door handle and was just on the point of getting out when the heavy portals above me opened as if automatically. There emerged a slightly built man with a thin, sharp face sporting square black glasses. His mousey hair had been carefully combed back without a parting. He appeared to be in his late thirties. His black butler's jacket hung rather limply from his shoulders and his pin-striped trousers ballooned around his slim waist. He began carefully to descend the steps in front of the house. By the time he reached my car,

I was already standing beside it. He addressed me in a soft lilt.

'Lady Hildreth? Mr Lockhart is expecting you. May I show you inside?'

When I entered the large marble-floored hall, Marvin was standing alone in the middle of the room. His statuesque figure blended well with the style of the house. As soon as he saw me, he moved forward, his arm outstretched.

'Jane,' he said. 'This is nice. So good of you to make it. I know what a hassle it must have been for you to do battle with all that traffic out of London.' His voice echoed around the empty hall.

'I must admit I nearly didn't make it.'

'By golly, I'm glad you did.' The relief in his voice seemed to be genuine.

'So am I,' I said, holding out my hand. 'It's good to see you again, Marvin, after all this time. Simon will be sad to have missed the occasion.'

He hesitated. For a moment I thought he was going to ask me who Simon was. Then he said, 'Yes, well, before we join the others, I think I should tell you a little of what this is all about.'

He was taller than I remembered him, certainly over six feet. His well-cut grey hair was parted to the right. His white moustache had been trimmed to precisely the length of his upper lip. As he spoke, he inclined his head slightly to one side. That, and the firmness of his green eyes, gave him an air of total self-assurance, although this could have been deceptive. His voice was deep and measured. He wore well-pressed dark grey trousers and a blazer that had clearly been tailored to fit his well-shaped torso. A bright yellow silk handkerchief cascaded from his top pocket. A straw trilby would have completed the picture of 1920s elegance. Simon and I had guessed his age to be sixty-five. Looking at him now, I felt that the slight folds under his eyes might indicate that he was a little older.

'Are they all hunting, fishing, and shooting types?' I asked.

For a moment he looked mystified.

'Who?'

'Your guests.'

'Oh no.' He seemed relieved. 'No, no, none of them are. They may do that stuff in their spare time, but that's not why they're here. The reference to shooting in the invitation was a front, I'm afraid. No, the purpose here is very different. Everyone you will meet this evening has a professional interest in the design, manufacture, or purchase of military weapons. I've come over to try to sell my latest aircraft to your government. Not the best time to choose, I must admit, just when the cold war is over. But they have kindly allowed me to house one of the prototypes down the road at RAF Brize Norton.'

'And why me?' I asked. 'I don't buy or sell military weapons.'

He looked at me directly and paused for a moment. When he spoke he lowered his voice so that for the first time I had to strain to hear him.

'There is no point in beating about the bush. I know who your employers are,' he said. I cannot recollect exactly how I reacted to this; I suspect I just smiled. At any rate, he was not to be put off. There was a sharpness in his voice when he suddenly asked, 'Did you ever hear of the Star Wars deaths?'

I thought for a moment. The phrase certainly rang a bell. Then it came back to me. I had once seen a file with that title. Inside there had been listed the names of twenty-two British defence scientists, each of whom had died before his natural time. The first of these deaths had been an accident in 1982 when a computer scientist from a government defence research establishment had apparently driven his car over a steep embankment on to a disused railway line. The most recent had been a suicide in 1988, when a senior engineer working on a defence contract for a large 'electronics company had been found dead in his garden shed with electric wires running from his body to the mains.

There had been reasonably satisfactory explanations attached to all these deaths. Taken individually, there had been nothing really remarkable about any of them, although I seemed to remember that on at least three occasions the coroners had given open verdicts. The collective picture was, however, rather more disturbing. The sheer number of pretty similar cases was itself peculiar. It had certainly attracted the attention of the national press, as, indeed, it had of the department of government for which I worked.

Try as they might, however, my colleagues had not managed so far to establish any clear link between the deaths, other than the obvious: that each had taken place in and around British defence research establishments. The sensitivity of the work of the men who had died had varied enormously. Some of them had had connections with the U.S. Star Wars project. It was for this reason that we had allowed the CIA to look at the file. As it turned out, the Company had been no more successful in establishing any meaningful pattern than we had been. The dossier, now named 'Star Wars Deaths' by the CIA, had been left open on both sides of the Atlantic.

'Yes, I have heard of the Star Wars deaths,' I told

Marvin. 'But what have they to do with my invitation to your party?'

Marvin Lockhart looked at me intently for a moment. Then he said, 'I wouldn't want any of the gentlemen you are going to meet to be added to that list.' The sparkle had gone out of his eyes. The room seemed to feel colder than when I had entered it.

'I see,' I said slowly. 'Perhaps you had better tell me a little more about your guests and what they and you are really doing here.'

He bowed. 'I think so too,' he said.

# 3

The first thing that was clear as I entered the long, rectangular drawing room was that I was the only woman present. This no doubt explained why the buzz of quiet chatter faded away as I made my appearance. I didn't form the impression that the proceedings had been a wild party before my arrival. What is a fact is that when I came in, the room fell into virtual silence. There must have been about a dozen men clustered together in the centre of a space large enough to accommodate ten times as many. An elaborate chandelier swung precariously over their heads; packed in around them and having the effect of fencing surrounding a racecourse paddock was a jumble of sofas, side tables, and expensive-looking gilt chairs.

As we approached this group, Marvin's deep American voice shattered the silence.

'This is Lady Jane Hildreth, everybody. Jane, honey, let me introduce you first to Sir Anthony Dean, Permanent Secretary at the Ministry of Defence. They don't come much more senior than Sir Anthony.'

As it happened, I knew Marvin was right. In the pecking order of Whitehall officialdom, Sir Anthony Dean was second only in importance to the cabinet secretary, who was also head of the Civil Service. Because of the length of time he had held the position of permanent secretary, he ranked, at least informally, above the head of the Foreign Service. Whatever his precise placing in the established order, Sir Anthony was a very powerful man indeed. There were certainly very few cabinet ministers who would have dared to make an enemy of him. His strength lay not just in his title, but every bit as much in the force of his personality. It was rumoured that even the Prime Minister was wary of him.

By coincidence, Sir Anthony knew me. I had once carried out an assignment for him when he had been a Deputy Secretary responsible for liaison between the Ministry of Defence and MI5. For a short time I had, in fact, been the main link between his office and my department. His powerful square shoulders, chubby face, and almost totally bald head had earned him the nickname of 'Boxer Dean'. I had always thought that this was rather apt. He certainly had more the appearance of a prize fighter than a civil servant. What's more, infighting was certainly his speciality. Rather unusually for someone in his profession, his weapon tended to be the spoken bludgeon rather than the written rapier. His ability to choose his words and to use them to maximum effect did not, I suspect, make him particularly popular with his peers.

I have to say that on this occasion his response to Marvin's introduction could not have been more genial. He broke away immediately from the closed circle of men and hurried over to greet me. There was nothing awesome in his voice when he said, 'Thank God the evening's not turning out to be a stag party after all. Nice to see you again, Jane, and looking, if I may say so, as bonny as ever. You didn't tell me her ladyship was coming, Marvin. To think I almost had to make my excuses and cry off. If I may ask, is this business or pleasure?'

His voice was low pitched and forceful, but it was unclear whether the question had been addressed to Marvin or to me. Marvin chose to answer it.

'Speaking personally, it's her delightful company that counts.' Evidently he had lost none of his smoothness during the past year.

The senior civil servant responded, as I might have hoped he would not, with a wink. I decided this required an instant antidote.

'Marvin and I met last year in Florida when I was on holiday there with a friend.'

Whatever Sir Anthony made of this, it had the desired effect of encouraging him to change the subject.

'Everyone here knows about Marvin's new aeroplane, so I imagine you do, too?' His smile faded as he addressed the question to me.

'I know there is such a thing,' I responded carefully.

'She also knows that I'm trying my darnedest to sell it to you,' Marvin intervened.

Sir Anthony produced a silver cigarette case from his inside pocket and flicked it open with his right hand.

'You don't smoke, if I remember, Jane?'

'Not at all.'

'I think you're going to have to be more careful, Marvin. Until we've had a chance to take a proper look at your machine, you really shouldn't talk about our interest to all and sundry'.

He drew a lighter from the left-hand pocket of his jacket and lit his cigarette.

'I'm sure you understand I don't get the budgets for new assets that I used to. If my political masters were to believe that I was jumping the gun, or, more important, that you were, your proposal would be killed off before our negotiations had even begun.'

Marvin stared at him for a moment, apparently weighing up how best to respond. If I had been him, I would have done so as compliantly as possible.

In fact, he said, 'I'm sorry, Anthony. I hadn't thought of Jane as all and sundry, as you put it. On the contrary, I had assumed she was part of the charmed circle.' This sounded to me needlessly provocative.

Sir Anthony blew away the smoke from his cigarette and looked straight into the face of the American. I sensed a definite tension between the two men and was surprised that Marvin, as the would-be seller, had allowed this to come about.

'That brings us back to what she's doing here,' Sir Anthony said. 'I'm still a little unclear on that.'

'I take your point, sir.' Marvin bowed slightly. I was unsure whether this was some sort of a retreat. It certainly didn't seem to appease Sir Anthony, who continued to stare coldly at him. I began to wonder whether this apparent friction between them had deeper roots than the present conversation.

'Will you forgive me, Anthony,' I heard Marvin say, 'if I take the lady over to meet some of my other guests?'

Sir Anthony appeared to ignore him. He turned sharply to me and said, 'Jane, I would very much welcome a private natter with you before you leave.'

Marvin led me by the elbow deeper into the room.

'I'm sorry about that,' he said. 'Now I want you to meet the two men who really understand what my new aeroplane is all about.'

'What's it called?' I asked.

'My aeroplane?'

'Yes.'

He laughed, partly, I felt, in relief to be away from Sir Anthony Dean.

'You know, that's one of the darnedest things. It is by far my greatest and most creative invention so far, and every serious government should have squadrons and squadrons of them, and yet I can't fix on a name which does full justice to its qualities. I simply call it GS1, which stands for Ground Support 1, because that is what it is: more a flying tank than an aeroplane. Now let me introduce you to Guy Simmonds of the Royal Signals and Radar Establishment at Malvern.'

I found myself looking up into the face of a man who was somehow too good looking to be a scientist. His swarthy face had the appearance of an Italian opera singer. His shiny black hair was brushed back flat over his well-rounded head. His dark intelligent eyes stared straight into mine.

He held out a hand and said, 'Hello. I'm Guy. You must be the Jane Hildreth that Marvin goes on about.'

Marvin grinned paternalistically beside me.

'Hello, Guy,' I said, holding his hand. 'And what part do you play in all of this?'

Guy looked for a moment at Marvin, who nodded.

'My job is to test the GS1 for its radar penetration capabilities.'

'Just that,' I said quietly.

For a moment he looked rather hurt. He wrinkled his elegant nose; then he laughed.

'I don't know how much you know about this

machine, but radar penetration is what it's meant to be all about.'

'That's right,' Marvin said, 'since it's a ground-support weapon, it has to be effective at slow speeds. That means it has to be very well armoured, and I mean armoured like a flying tank. So you can understand the importance of its radar avoidance capabilities. Guy's job is to make sure that I am not pulling the wool over Her Majesty's Government's eyes.'

'And how long will your assessments take?' I asked.

'The flight trials are scheduled for two months, and after that, who knows?'

I found the intensity in Guy's voice distinctly interesting.

'Come and meet someone else,' Marvin said. It was as if he had anticipated that I was about to start enjoying myself; evidently this was not included in his plan.

'I want you to meet Dr Leatherhead. He may leave any minute. I know he has to get to a meeting. It is important that you should talk to him before he leaves. Ah, there you are, Tom. Meet Lady Jane Hildreth from the security services. Jane, Tom is an aeronautical engineer who teaches at the Royal Military Academy of Science at Shrivenham. He has been commissioned by your government to lead the team looking at the aerodynamic properties of GS1. It's a very heavy aeroplane and I have to persuade the world that it can be operated economically and with stability.'

Dr Leatherhead did not appear to be in the best of health. Sweat was pouring from both sides of his face; his cheeks were flushed; he was clearly overweight. He seemed to need to breathe in deeply through his mouth before he spoke. When finally he uttered, his words were interspersed with the crackle of bronchial catarrh. His eyes were little slits hidden behind the puffiness of his cheeks.

'You may not recognize me, Lady Hildreth, but I remember you very well,' he wheezed. I must have looked a little startled by this introduction. 'We worked together indirectly on the bomb they found a few years ago on the British Airways 747. As I recollect, it wasn't entirely by chance that you were a passenger on board and played some part in talking around the poor sod who was meant to activate the weapon. I was an adviser at the enquiry they held afterwards. We didn't actually meet formally, but your name was very prominent at the time.'

'I remember the event, of course,' I said.

'What, if I may ask, are you doing here?' His question was sharp and direct, almost rude.

'I'm not quite sure yet,' I replied, with honesty.

At this his eyes seemed to close altogether. For a moment I thought he had fallen asleep on his feet. Somewhat disconcerted, I began to look around for Marvin. For the first time since my arrival, he seemed to have deserted me. I decided in the circumstances to make a unilateral move away from the apparently somnolent scientist. Just as I was on the point of making the break, he opened his eyes wide. For the first time I saw that they were very bloodshot.

'It's about flaming time you security people became involved in this business,' he said. 'As it is, you're probably too late. Where have you all been for the past few weeks?'

I was too experienced not to try to play the role he clearly expected of me.

'We're not perfect,' I conceded. 'It's even possible you may be ahead of us.'

He screwed up his eyes again as if shutting out the sheer incompetence of the world outside.

He sighed and said, 'You want to talk to Simmonds. He probably knows even more than I do.'

'Guy Simmonds?'

'Of course, from the RSRE Malvern. He and I are the joint assessors for the GS1. He's here somewhere.'

'I know; I have just met him.'

He shrugged his shoulders. 'In that case you probably know it all already,' he sighed.

'Let's get him over,' I suggested, with what I hoped was sufficiently disguised enthusiasm.

'Can you see him?' he asked. 'My eyesight isn't as good as it used to be.'

'I'll find him and bring him over,' I said.

I left Dr Leatherhead and made a quick survey of the room. Had he been there, I would have been able to pick out Mr Simmonds immediately. His height and the small number of people present would have made him totally conspicuous. Manifestly he had just left the room. I hurried to the door that led into the hall. As I did so, a hand from behind fell heavily on my shoulder.

'Not going already, I hope?' Sir Anthony Dean enquired. 'You haven't forgotten about our little chat?' This time his deep, gruntlike voice had a slight menace to it.

'No, I'm not leaving, Sir Anthony, but I must find Guy Simmonds.'

The permanent secretary relaxed and smiled. 'Oh, it's like that, is it? You should catch him in the hall. He left only a few moments ago. Good-looking chap, Guy Simmonds, and definitely a high flyer. He might even be the first scientist to hold my job if he plays his cards right. You've got good taste, Jane. I'll see you when you come back.'

I chose to ignore all this, accompanied as it was by one of his now all-too-familiar winks. I headed straight for the door. The hall outside was deserted. As I ran across it to the main entrance, I was conscious once again of the echo, on this occasion made by the sound of the heels of my shoes clattering over the marble floor.

I pushed open the heavy oak door and was just in time to see a red convertible sportscar race away down the drive and into the gloom. The driver's black hair trailed in the wind behind him.

Suddenly I was aware that I was not alone. I half-turned and looked straight into the face of a man whom I had not previously spotted amongst the guests. He was shorter than me, and I am not tall. He wore thick spectacles, behind which his eyes flickered like a light bulb on the point of going out. His hair was grey and curly and fell in little ringlets down the back of his neck.

At first he said nothing, his attention apparently absorbed by the sight of the disappearing car. When it was completely out of sight, he let out a sigh. Then, suddenly, as if noticing me for the first time, he asked in a surprisingly firm voice, 'How well do you know him?'

'If we're talking about Guy Simmonds, I met him for the first time this evening.'

The man next to me seemed relieved.

'Attractive fellow, don't you think? I was hoping to catch him before he left. I'll have to see him in the office tomorrow.'

'You are colleagues at RSRE Malvern?'

For a moment he appeared to be strangely taken

aback by this innocent question. He seemed to feel the need to consider its implications carefully before responding. There was a definite pause before he said, 'Yes, yes; we work on aviation matters together. My name is Masters, Philip Masters. And yours?'

I was on the point of replying when a sudden, urgent shout came from the hall behind us. A familiar American voice ordered, 'Get a goddamned doctor, quick.'

Masters and I collided briefly as we turned around simultaneously to face the house. Through the front door I could make out Marvin Lockhart's distinguished figure as it stood erect in the middle of the hall. The only gesticulation he made was a slight movement with the right arm.

'What's happening?' I called out to him as I came through the door.

'Dr Leatherhead has collapsed,' he shouted back. 'I think he may be dead.'

# 4

The scene back in the living room had been dramatically transformed from the one I had left a few minutes earlier. Dr Leatherhead was lying on his back on the floor. Around him, the remainder of the guests stood motionless in a circle, nobody apparently knowing how to help him. I heard Marvin shout to one of the staff who had been serving drinks to ring for the local doctor. I pushed my way through the little crowd and knelt down beside the unconscious scientist. One look at him told me he was still breathing. I undid his tie and collar and pressed two fingers against each side of his Adam's apple. His pulse was very weak. Placing both my hands on top of each other at the base of his rib cage, I began to pump rhythmically. After a few moments, I realized that this was not going to be enough to save his life; his breathing was becoming weaker. I held his nose, put my lips to his mouth, and breathed into his lungs. Slowly, at last, I began to feel life return to his body. After a few minutes, his eyes opened; they stared up at me, bloodshot and grateful. He moved his mouth and tried to say something. I put my fingers to my lips and he seemed to recognize this as a signal to him to conserve his energy.

'I'm not medically qualified,' I said, 'but it looks as

though Dr Leatherhead may have had a slight stroke. The main thing now is to keep him warm until the doctor arrives.'

Relieved to be able to help at last, everyone began simultaneously to strip off his jacket.

As I began to stand up, my eyes met those of Sir Anthony. He held a tulip-shaped champagne glass towards me.

'This will do you a lot of good,' he said, speaking quietly and almost without moving his lips. 'I wonder if you would mind coming over here into a corner, Jane. I want to try to avoid being overheard.'

I looked down at Dr Leatherhead. His eyes were closed, but there was colour in his cheeks. The butler had begun to fuss around him with a large woollen rug, which he tucked carefully under Dr Leatherhead's sides.

'All right,' I said, 'but I would like to be around when the doctor arrives.'

I followed the permanent secretary to the far side of the room. We sat down on two gilt chairs out of earshot of the others.

'The first thing I want to say,' he began, 'and it's for your ears only, Jane, is that there isn't a cat in hell's chance of our buying your friend Marvin's aeroplane. It might have had its uses if we were preparing to fight a land war in central Europe, but all that's gone out of the window, at least for the time being. If the Russians turn nasty again, which they might well do, then we'll have to think of something new.'

'So why string Marvin along?' I asked. 'Wouldn't it be kinder just to tell him you don't want his aeroplane?'

Sir Anthony Dean's whole manner was beginning

to irritate me. I had no doubt that Marvin's enthusiasm needed to be reined in a little, but that was no reason for engaging in an act of calculated deception against him. Being the astute civil servant that he was, Sir Anthony was immediately sensitive to my annoyance.

'Let me try to explain,' he said, with a newfound softness. 'There are two reasons why we can't be too blunt about this. First, we don't want to be thought to be dismantling our defence plans too hastily. That could have the unfortunate effect of sending all the wrong signals around the world, especially to the Americans, who rather naturally want us to do more, not less, for ourselves in Europe. Secondly, and rather more significantly from the point of view of this conversation, we want to find out a little more about Mr Lockhart before we say good-bye to him forever. We can't make him out at all. He must know that in the changed circumstances, we won't buy; he's an intelligent man. And yet he persists in putting in all this extraordinary effort. The base he has set up over here is quite something. So what's he up to? What has he rented this palatial house for? It doesn't quite add up at the moment. I am beginning to wonder whether this is all part of a diversionary operation to hide something else he's up to.'

He waited for my reaction.

'Or it could simply be his vanity,' I suggested. Sir Anthony raised an eyebrow, which was surprisingly bushy, given the lack of hair on his head. 'Marvin seems to get a kick out of showing off his aeroplanes even when there isn't much chance of selling them. He just likes them to be talked about.'

Sir Anthony considered this for a moment. Then he said, 'As military equipment is involved, we shall have to keep an eye on him. I think you may be misjudging the situation.'

The last sentence was said coldly; all trace of gentleness had once again disappeared from his voice. There was also a certainty in his manner that in the circumstances I found surprising. It occurred to me that he might have information that he was not passing over to me.

'What do you want me to do about it, Sir Anthony?'

He gave me a long hard look. Knowing now what occurred afterward, I imagine he was considering very carefully how best he should proceed.

'Just keep in touch with Lockhart. Officially, I mean.'

'Is that all?'

'Not quite.'

I hoped he wasn't going to be too long-winded. I would need to give my undivided attention to Dr Leatherhead when the doctor arrived. I certainly wanted to be around to hear anything he might say that would explain his previous agitation.

I heard Sir Anthony say, 'Have you ever come across the Star Wars Deaths file?'

I began to concentrate on him in a way that I had not before.

'That's the second time I've been asked that question in the last hour,' I said.

'Really?' His surprise seemed genuine. 'Who else has raised it?'

'Marvin Lockhart, as a matter of fact.'

This time there was no doubting his shock.

'Good God.' His thick shoulders slumped forward. A tiny globule of sweat formed beneath his right ear and then began to roll down the side of his neck.

'I must admit I thought it a little odd that he should

know about such a sensitive dossier,' I said. 'It was one of the things I planned to look into when I got back to the office.'

The civil servant's head was now bent, its bald top reflecting the lights of the chandelier. We sat in silence for several moments. When he looked up, his steely blue eyes were weary.

'I think you should study that file again.' He spoke slowly and with deliberation. He seemed to be choosing his words carefully. 'If you were to do so, I believe you would find certain clear patterns which you may have missed before. If, for instance, you were to analyse the deaths by place of work, not the most sophisticated of tasks, you would find that, with one or two exceptions, the scientists fitted into one of two categories: those who were employed by the private sector and those who were associated with either the Royal Military College of Science or RSRE Malvern.'

'Where Guy Simmonds and Dr Leatherhead come from?'

'Yes.'

'Coincidentally?'

'I doubt it.'

'You have more information?'

'Of course.'

'Which is shared with my department?'

'I don't know.'

'But you have your own sources?'

'Yes.'

I knew that one should never underestimate the impregnability of the boundaries between Whitehall departments. Nowhere did this seem to be more true than between the Ministry of Defence and my department.

'Well, that's that,' I said.

Just as I was about to get up to go, he placed a hand on my arm. His fingers were thick and stubby, the forefinger stained by nicotine.

'Wait,' he said, 'we may be able to come to an arrangement.'

I sat back in my chair.

He looked directly at me as he continued. 'For some reason that I do not fully comprehend, the Ministry of Defence does not possess a copy of the Star Wars Deaths file. This makes it impossible for me to carry out an independent assessment of its contents. That is something which you will already have gathered I would very much like to do. If you can secure a copy for me, Jane, I will promise to let you have the full results of my study, including all the premises and sources.'

'Sounds interesting,' I said. 'I'll check back with the Director General.'

'Do you think he will cooperate?' I detected a new note of anxiety in his voice.

'Possibly,' I said. Reflecting on my aborted conversation with Dr Leatherhead, I thought it quite possible that the chief might be sufficiently interested in this matter to bargain with Sir Anthony in the way that had been suggested.

'Does he take your advice?' he asked.

'Sometimes.'

Sir Anthony gave me a sly sideways look that I did not appreciate.

'The DG takes your advice, does he?'

'Sometimes,' I repeated.

# 5

The Honourable Patricia Huntington raised a white china teapot with its Crown Derby 'Posy' design of pink and yellow wildflowers. She began to pour the tea slowly into cups that matched the pot. I watched her through half-closed eyes from where I lay stretched out on my back on the lawn, my head resting on an old Indian silk cushion. My mother would have had a small 'turn' had she been able to see me now, not because of the scantiness of my bikini (she had come to accept seminudity before she died) but because of the abuse of a cushion. For my mother, cushions had been works of art to be viewed from afar, ranged and puffed up on distant and unassailable sofas, preferably remaining forever unsullied by the human behind. Even as she had lain dying on a chaise longue in the middle of her living room, she had seemed to be slightly ashamed to be 'spoiling the cushions'. My mother had had great style.

'Shall I bring it over?' Pat called out.

'Wonderful,' I mumbled. 'I really ought to get up. The sun is quite burning. Look how scorched the lawn has become over the last few days. I imagine Jim hasn't had to mow it for weeks.'

'Jim hasn't been here for weeks. I think he's got a new contract to look after the churchyard. You'll probably have to pay him some more money if you want him back.'

'I'll leave that to you, Pat. As usual, I probably won't be around long enough to sort it out. Give him whatever it takes to make him happy. I couldn't bear the garden to go to rack and ruin just for the lack of a few pennies.'

Pat deposited a cup and saucer on the grass beside me and sat herself down close by.

'I never did like the sun much,' she confessed, 'though God knows I've been in hot enough places in my time. My skin's too pale for it.'

I think it must have been the first time I ever heard her admit to any physical weakness. Her next sentence was, for her, if anything even more extraordinary.

'The roses seem to thrive in this hot weather; the second crop is even more beautiful than the first.'

I lifted myself on to one elbow and looked at her closely. She had never mentioned her appreciation of any flower before, let alone roses.

'Everything all right, Pat?' I asked as casually as possible.

'Could be worse,' was her noncommittal reply.

Something was not quite right. Pat Huntington had left it a bit late to start acquiring an interest in country gardens. Much better that she should carry on tinkering under the chassis of her still-growing collection of vintage cars.

Until her sixty-fifth birthday, Pat had been one of the department's frontline agents. She had never forgiven those who had been responsible for pensioning her off. Nor had she ever let up in her campaign to persuade me to press her case for being recalled to active duty. One of her stronger arguments for this was that she claimed still to be the best small-arms marksman in the 'office'. I would not have been totally surprised to discover that this was true. Some ten years earlier she had certainly taught me most of what I knew about armed combat. What was also a fact was that she did not consider guarding my cottage in Chipping Campden as any sort of an adequate use of her talents – and she was probably right.

As if reading my thoughts, she said, 'Don't you honestly think I've rested for long enough?'

I sighed. 'My dear Pat, we've been over this so many times. I can't alter the fact that, rightly or wrongly – probably the latter – company policy is to be very sparing in the use of seventy-something-year-old ladies, however brilliant they are at fighting the nation's enemies.' (Pat was just as good at unarmed combat as she was with guns.)

She didn't seem to have been paying much attention to me.

'It wouldn't need to be for too long: six months in the desert would do quite nicely. That's where all the wars are fought these days, isn't it? But I'd settle for a good jungle.'

I laughed a little nervously. I found it hard to gauge how serious she was being.

'I'll have a go,' I said. 'I'll try to arrange for you to come on the next decent foreign assignment.'

The strange thing was that I meant it. Certainly the promise seemed to humour her. She pushed back several strands of white hair. Now it was her turn to sigh. It seemed to indicate a new contentment. At that moment the telephone rang.

'I'll get it,' she said.

When she reemerged from the house, she had a satisfied look on her face.

'That's settled,' she said. 'You're fixed to have lunch tomorrow with those two scientists. That was Mrs Leatherhead to confirm that her husband is sufficiently recovered to be able to make it. Apparently he's looking forward to the occasion.'

It was a relief to hear that Dr Leatherhead would be well enough to see me tomorrow since he had been too ill to talk to me at Giddlington Manor at the end of Marvin's party. And I was glad that it was going to be a joint meeting with Guy Simmonds. It might be necessary to interview each separately at a later stage. For the moment it would help to see them together.

'Did Mrs Leatherhead give any more details about her husband's health?' I asked.

'Apparently he spent the night before last in hospital, but is pretty well all right now. I've arranged for lunch for you all at the Lygon Arms Hotel in Broadway.'

'That won't be cheap,' I said. 'We'd better arrange for the bill to be sent here. I doubt whether Accounts in the office will want to receive it. They're much more snooty about these things than they used to be – preparing for the day when all our books are opened to public scrutiny, I suppose.'

'What does Guy Simmonds look like?' Pat's question came rather out of the blue. 'He sounded rather sexy on the phone when he rang this morning. He was very perky about seeing you again.'

'He *is* sexy,' I admitted.

'Ah.'

'But then,' I added hastily, 'I'm not, as they say, a free agent.'

'Simon still bothering you?'

'We're thinking of getting married, if that's what you mean.' This sounded harsher than I had meant.

'That would be a pity,' she said, rather sniffily.

'You're jealous,' I replied.

For the first time since lunch she laughed, and I was much relieved that at last she seemed to be returning to normal. Gone, I hoped for good, would be the talk of roses. From anyone else, yes, but not from Pat Huntington.

'You're right,' she said. 'I probably am a bit jealous. I never had an awful lot of time for sex when I was young. I suppose I was too busy fighting the war. There were a lot of men around, of course, perhaps too many. It was very difficult to get serious with any one of them. Anyway, they kept coming and going the whole time, and then every so often one of them was inconsiderate enough to get himself killed.'

I looked closely at her. She must once have been very pretty indeed. Certainly the signs of beauty were still there: the high cheekbones, large black gypsy eyes, soft translucent skin, and long white strands of hair that must once have been jet black and which still sometimes fell coquettishly across her forehead. Her figure was a little too thin for my liking. (I once told her of my worries about how little she ate. Her response of 'Like the SAS' had not been much comfort.) When she had been young, the slimness of her body must have been enormously attractive.

'Where exactly do I meet these two chaps?' I asked.

'They'll wait for you in the lounge by the courtyard at the back of the hotel,' she said.

# 6

Four men in tennis whites sat at a table not far from me. They were discussing an apparently proposed bypass to be built around the village of Broadway. One of them, a large, oval-faced man, seemed to be quite upset by this prospect. 'It's all very well, but it's my bloody house it will go through,' he exclaimed.

The man on his left replied quietly, 'Without it the village will fall down in a pile of rubble. The place is being shaken to its foundations by lorries.'

In front of each man was placed a Pimm's glass, now almost empty except for sodden pieces of cucumber rind and orange and leaves of mint at the bottom. The youngest of them, in his late thirties, with long dark hair and a droopy moustache, looked over in my direction. I couldn't tell whether this was out of pity that I was still on my own or out of hope that I might come over and divert the conversation to a different subject.

I looked at my watch: one-forty. I had been waiting for almost an hour.

Suddenly the men on the next table rose in unison. 'The Pimm's was better than the game,' the younger man said, 'but thanks for both.'

The bypass protester gave a loud whistle and wiped

the sweat from his forehead with the back of his arm. 'My God, it's almost two o'clock. My wife will kill me when I get home. She was cooking lunch for half past one.'

They picked up their tennis racquets and drifted off into the recesses of the hotel. When they had disappeared, I got up and went through to the reception lobby. I dialled Pat Huntington's number from a public phone.

'They haven't shown up,' I said. 'Are you quite sure you made it for today? It seems a bit odd that they should both have forgotten. I haven't been stood up like this for quite a while. Quite embarrassing, as a matter of fact. There was a group of locals sitting near me. One of them who was vaguely familiar kept giving me the eye.'

'I'm a hundred per cent certain I said today.' Pat didn't sound too worried. 'I'll ring their offices to see what on earth happened,' she added. 'Hang on by the phone by the hotel reception desk, Jane; I'll come back right away.'

The phone beside me rang about five minutes later. This time Pat was more concerned.

'It's very odd,' she said. 'I got hold of both Dr Leatherhead's office and Mr Simmonds's. Both the secretaries were very nice. They confirmed that the appointments were for lunch today. But that was all they knew. Neither Leatherhead nor Simmonds has been in any sort of contact with his office the whole morning. Normally both men would have been expected to look in before going on to meet you. Neither, apparently, had any other outside appointments, at least not according to their office diaries.'

'There could have been an accident,' I suggested.

'It's possible,' Pat agreed, 'but as they would have

been travelling in separate cars, there would have to have been two.'

'Have you tried their homes?' I asked.

'Irritatingly, neither office would give me a home number. I shall have to go through the department. I'm afraid it's all going to take rather more time.'

'In that case, I'll come home,' I said, 'and join in the search from there. I'll leave a message with the receptionist here in case either of them turns up. From what you have said, that doesn't sound very likely.'

I left the hotel by the back entrance. My car was parked behind a garden and next to a tennis court. I drove through the hotel arch and turned left on the main street. Once out of the village, the road climbed steeply into the Cotswolds. Below me to the right, the county of Hereford and Worcester stretched flat, burnt by the summer sun, toward the horizon where a streak of blue marked the Malvern Hills. As I reached the top of Fish Hill, my car phone rang. It was Pat to say that there had been no reply from the home numbers.

'It's very frustrating,' I complained, 'I know so little about either of them. I couldn't even tell you whether Guy Simmonds is married.'

'He isn't.'

I thought I heard her chuckle, but it might have been static from the airwaves.

'I got it off Personnel in the Ministry of Defence. He lives with his mother.'

'When I get home, I think we had better contact the police,' I said.

'Isn't that a bit hasty?' she asked.

'Did you ever come across the Star Wars Deaths file, Pat?'

There was a pause. The static was getting worse. For a moment I thought we had been cut off.

'Are you still there?' I asked.

'I can't say it rings any bells,' I heard her say at last. 'It sounds a bit after my time. Remember it's been almost ten years since I was given the boot. I don't think we had ever heard of star wars in those days, except in films.'

When I arrived back at my cottage, I entered by the back door, which opened on to a narrow path at the side. Pat was sitting at the far end of the light oak table that occupied most of the centre of the kitchen. She had on the khaki dungarees she wore to service her cars. A green scarf was tied somewhat incongruously around her head in Indian-squaw fashion.

As I entered the room I sensed a definite air of tension. Pat's cheeks were unusually flushed. She had clearly been exerting herself. In front of her on the table lay my scrambler phone, which we used only in exceptional circumstances.

Beside the telephone was a reading light that Pat must have brought in from the living room. Although it was still mid-afternoon, she had clearly felt the need for greater illumination in my low-beamed old Cotswold house. All the signs were that something unexpected had happened during the ten minutes since we had last spoken.

'What's going on?' I asked.

'They're both dead.' There was a thrill to her voice that in other circumstances would have made what she said sound like some sort of message of triumph.

I sat down beside her. 'How do you know?' I demanded aggressively. I had liked the look of Guy Simmonds and had wanted to get to know him

49

better. The news of his death genuinely shocked me.

'Your friend Marvin Lockhart has just rung,' I heard Pat say.

'He told you that they were dead? How on earth did he know?'

'I think the police must have been on to him.'

'I wonder why. What about the cause of the deaths? Did Marvin say anything about that?'

'Dr Leatherhead apparently had another heart attack.'

'And Guy Simmonds?'

'He was found in his garage, sitting in his car with the engine running, one end of a hose pipe in his hand and the other end fixed to the exhaust.'

'Suicide?'

'That's apparently what the police are saying.'

I looked at Pat. Her eyes were alert and full of intelligence. 'Don't you think that's a bit strange,' I asked, 'their both dying on the same day?'

She shrugged. 'I've known bigger coincidences in my time.'

'Coincidence?' I repeated. 'Both on the same day and each a few hours before they were due to have lunch with me to explain why the security services needed to be more closely concerned with Marvin Lockhart's efforts to sell his aeroplane?'

Through the window I had a glimpse of Jim Bruntsford striding behind a lawnmower. Pat's bribe of £4 an hour had clearly been sufficient to entice him back from the graveyard. My embryonic thoughts about the economics of country living were suddenly cut short by the shrill call of the emergency telephone from the kitchen table. I picked up the receiver.

A familiar voice said, 'Hello, is that you, Jane?

These two murders have put the whole Lockhart business into a rather different orbit, haven't they?'

'Murders?'

'I assume they were murdered, don't you?' the chief asked.

'Are you making the same assumption about the rest of the Star Wars deaths, sir?'

'I haven't come to any conclusion about them yet. Needless to say, I'm crawling over the file myself now. It's all very strange. These are the first two deaths to which we can attach any rational motive for murder.'

'Which is?'

'Most immediately, to stop you from having lunch with them.'

'A bit drastic, wasn't it, Chief?'

'Have you any better ideas?'

'No, but I may have some more information. May I come and tell you about something Sir Anthony Dean said to me when I bumped into him the other day?'

'By all means. But I think you should give Mr Lockhart a proper going over first, don't you?'

'Is that a relocation from Russian duties?' I asked hurriedly.

'Why do women always have to be so formal about these things?' he grumbled. 'The main point, Jane, is to be careful with Lockhart. I want to talk to you about him when you get back to the office. I wouldn't give him any warning that you are coming to see him, if I were you.'

'Just show up on the doorstep?'

'That's what I would do, but you must decide for yourself. You're the one on the spot.'

The chief had a habit of pretending to delegate while making the decisions that mattered himself.

51

'I'll leave for Little Giddlington in a few minutes,' I said.

Hearing this, Pat made her move. 'Right,' she said, 'I'd better come with you. You'll need a driver.'

This offer had one advantage. It meant that if we arrived alive, we would do so in half the time it would take a normal driver.

'We'll take the Buick,' she said, warming to the plan. 'It hasn't had a good go for months. Do you know, I once got seventy miles an hour out of it down High Street in Oxford.'

I shuddered with apprehension. If the Buick had done seventy mph down Oxford High Street, the mind boggled at what it would achieve along the twisting single-track lanes of the Cotswold Hills.

As a matter of fact, the twenty-odd-minute journey passed by pleasantly enough because throughout its passage I kept my eyes firmly closed and thought of Simon.

We reached the front steps of Giddlington Manor to find the whole place totally deserted. Very much in contrast to my previous visit only three days earlier, there was not a car to be seen on the gravelled drive.

'I think you had better stay here,' I said to Pat. She jerked up the thumb of her left hand as no doubt she had been taught to do by some parachute instructor at the time of the Battle of Arnhem.

'I'll keep the engine ticking over, just in case.' Her eyes were twinkling with enthusiasm.

I climbed the steps to the double doors and pulled on a brass bell lever. Above me a brace of squawking ducks flew toward the lake. Below on the drive, Pat manoeuvred the old car into position for what she would no doubt have described as 'a quick getaway'.

Beyond the thick oak doors there seemed to be no sign of life, so I rang again. Now, somewhere in the recesses of the building, I thought I could hear a muffled shuffling sound. To my relief this grew louder until it became the distinctive echo of feet crossing the marble floor of the hall. Then there was a rattle of bolts being withdrawn. Whoever was performing this operation was badly out of training. His breathing was heavy and came in irregular bursts.

When eventually the door was opened, it was the butler who put his head through the opening. He was tieless and without his jacket, and his chin was covered in short black stubble. For a moment I couldn't think what it was that was missing about him. Then I realized that he wasn't wearing his glasses.

'What do you want?' His voice was higher pitched than I remembered it and its tone was certainly less courteous than when we had last met. His slight accent was hard to make out; it seemed to come from somewhere between Birmingham and Leeds.

'I've come to see Mr Lockhart,' I said.

'Do you have an appointment?'

'No, but I've come on a matter of some urgency. I think he will wish to see me.'

The butler's reaction to this was to secure a chain across the inside of the door, making it impossible for me to force my way in. For a moment there was silence, then he said, 'He's not here.'

'What does that mean?' I asked. 'He still lives here, doesn't he?'

'He's gone away and that's what I advise you to do.'

'Can you at least tell me when he left?' I asked.

'This morning.'

If that were true, Marvin must have departed before

his manservant had had a chance to shave. I had to assume that in the normal course of events the American would not tolerate the present slovenly appearance of the man. Either Marvin Lockhart had left the day before, or in some haste early that morning. There was the interesting question of where he had been when he had telephoned Pat about an hour and a half earlier.

'Did he say where he was going?' I persisted.

'No.'

'What about when he was coming back?'

He shrugged and said, 'I'm going to close the door now. Good-bye, lady.'

The time had come to try to find out a little more about the man's attitude toward his employer.

'You realize that he may now be in grave danger?' I asked.

For the first time he looked straight at me. I could see his eyes were red and troubled. It was as if they had been weeping. When he spoke, his voice was almost a whisper.

'Are you from the police?'

'Would that make any difference?' I asked.

'Yes, it does, because I don't trust the police. But if you're from the law, I suppose you'll have to come in. You probably have a warrant. If you haven't, no doubt you'll be able to get one.'

Evidently he had a firm grasp of police entry procedure. I looked behind me to make sure that Pat was in place and then said, 'Yes, I would like to come in, though I probably won't need to take up much of your time on this occasion.'

He withdrew the latch and opened the door wide enough for me to be able to enter the house.

'Let's talk here in the hall,' I suggested. 'It's Mr King, isn't it?'

Several oak chairs lined the wall on the far side. He turned two of these to face each other. As soon as we sat down, rather to my surprise, he began to speak unprompted.

'Look, madam, I genuinely haven't a clue where Mr Lockhart has gone to, though I'm as worried for him as you appear to be.'

'Why?' I asked with a directness that I immediately regretted. There was no doubt it put him off his stride. For a moment he stared at the floor in silence. Then, suddenly, he seemed to shake himself into action. It was as if he had needed to make some sort of clear decision about how to proceed.

'As you may know,' he said, 'all the staff are on contract here for the duration of Mr Lockhart's stay. That is to say, we are free-lance; it also means we get about the country a bit. That certainly goes for myself. I don't do many one-night stands, if you'll pardon the expression. I don't do parties unless they are part of a longer contract. I tend to work two- to three-month contracts and I go back regularly to the same clients when they are short-staffed. In recent years I have found myself on the military network. More and more of defence catering work is being contracted out these days and they don't seem to be able to get the right sort of butlering staff. So they use people like me at more or less regular intervals to fill in.'

I couldn't help wondering why he was telling me all this.

'One of the places that asks me back quite often is the Royal Military College at Shrivenham.'

'Did you come across Dr Leatherhead there?' I asked.

'Of course. He always took his lunch in the mess. Your next question will be, do I know that he is dead? The answer is that I do.'

He paused. When he spoke again, it was with much greater deliberation. There was a new firmness in his voice. 'If you hadn't been there the other night, he would probably have died then.'

'I think you're trying to tell me that his death was predictable?'

'It was certainly part of a pattern.'

'There have been other similar deaths?'

He stamped his right foot on the marble floor. His thin body, dressed only in jeans and a T-shirt, suddenly began to shake with apparent anger.

'Don't play around with me. You know damn well there have been other deaths, twenty-two of them to be precise. That's why you're here. Tom Leatherhead and Guy Simmonds are only the latest in the line which, as you suspect, may now stretch forward to include Marvin.'

The use of Lockhart's Christian name was surprising in the circumstances. I looked directly at him for a moment without speaking. I was beginning to wonder if Mr King had credentials over and perhaps above his butlering duties. His hair, which when we had met before had been groomed to the point of effeminacy, now hung in strands down the side of his thin face, lank and greasy. Two patches of sweat soiled his T-shirt on each side of his chest.

I said, 'I'm sorry I interrupted you. Do please go on.'

He seemed to hesitate. 'I wonder if I should,' he muttered.

'You must have had some reason for going this far,' I said.

Suddenly his eyes flared up again. 'The bastards,' he said. 'The filthy bastards.'

'Who?' I asked.

'The police. The filthy, lousy fuzz. They set up Guy Simmonds' so-called bloody suicide, just as they did Mike Sherwood's.'

'Mike Sherwood?'

'Dr Mike Sherwood, poor sod, one of the staff at Shrivenham. He was supposed to have killed himself with a handkerchief soaked in chloroform. But I don't bloody believe it, do you understand that, I don't bloody believe it.' He began to sob unashamedly.

'Why not?' I persisted.

'Because they wouldn't let me see him, that's why,' he shouted. 'We were lovers and they knew it. I had a right to see his body. I pleaded with them on my knees, but they surrounded his room with armed guards. It was terrible. Eventually they took him away in the middle of the night in a coffin. I watched them leave. I learned later that they transported him to a morgue controlled by the military; there eventually they cremated him. Some months later, I heard from a contact who had left the police that they had taken several photos of his body. I tried to get permission to see these. I even wrote to my local Member of Parliament about it.' He stopped crying. The steel returned to his voice. 'The authorities flatly refused to allow me to see them on the grounds that they would be too disturbing.'

'And what of the motives for the supposed cover-up?' I asked. 'You must have developed some theory as to what would make them want to operate in such an extraordinary way.'

He shrugged. 'How the hell should I know? The

guy was sitting on a pile of secrets. No doubt they thought that, as a gay, he was open to blackmail. Perhaps he was.' He put his head between his hands and stared angrily at the floor. 'But that was no reason to kill him, no bloody reason at all.'

'And you believe that Dr Leatherhead's death fits into the same pattern?' I asked.

Apparently brushing aside the question, he said, 'I will tell you two more things, and then you must make up your own bloody mind.'

'That may turn out to be somewhat optimistic.'

'I think you will find Philip Masters would repay a visit.'

'Philip Masters?' The name was familiar, but for a moment I couldn't place it.

'You met him at the party the other night. Side by side you watched the departure of Guy Simmonds.'

'Of course I remember, on the steps at Marvin's party, the little man with glasses from the Radar Establishment at Malvern.'

'I know he would be willing to discuss his experiences with you should you wish to hear them. You will find him pretty bitter, like me. It's too late to do anything now for his beloved Guy.'

It seemed that there existed quite an elaborate network of homosexuals around the government's defence research establishments.

'I'll follow your advice,' I said. 'I will certainly make contact with Dr Masters. I think you said there was a second point?' Suddenly he had become somewhat distant; for a moment I thought he wasn't listening. 'Mr King, you had another piece of information you wanted to give me.' I must admit I was still unclear as to why he had wanted to volunteer anything at all to me.

'Yes,' he said slowly, 'you seem to have forgotten why you called at Giddlington Manor in the first place. You were, I believe, looking for Marvin Lockhart.'

'And you assured me that you didn't have a clue where he was.'

'And that's true.'

'So?'

'But I may know who he's with.'

'Ah.'

'May I tell you?'

'Please.'

'He is probably with his woman.'

The last word exploded from his mouth with such venom that I resisted the temptation of asking which one. Instead I said, 'That means he's probably back in the United States.'

'It's possible, but I doubt it. She has been over here for the past few weeks.'

I sat up, for the first time genuinely interested.

'Why wasn't she at his party?' I asked.

'She hasn't been visible in public at all,' he said.

'But you have seen her?'

'It's more than that; I have felt her presence. I can always tell if there is a woman around a man I am attracted to. But yes, to answer your question directly, I have seen her. I have seen Ms Lucille Fraser all right, on several occasions over the last few weeks.'

I decided to try one 'flyer' question on him.

'Are you telling me that Lucille Fraser had something to do with Dr Leatherhead's death?'

'There we enter the realm of conjecture,' he said. 'I prefer to deal in facts, as I am sure you do, Lady Hildreth. But I wouldn't put anything past that woman. She is utterly ruthless, as I know to my cost.'

Pat Huntington was pacing nervously up and down beside the Buick as I ran out of the house and down the steps toward her.

'Get the Gloucestershire police on the car phone for me, please, Pat. Ask for the department's contact man there, Inspector Webb of Special Branch. I would like him to find out everything he can about Mr Alastair King, the butler here. He may need to pay him a visit. It would be especially interesting to find out whether Mr King has any record of violent behaviour. Once you are finished with Webb, will you try to make contact with Marvin's various houses in Florida? It's not very likely that he's heading back there, but we had better check on it. Meanwhile, I'll have a look at a map.'

## 7

Pat Huntington's 1934 Buick was not the most convenient place from which to try to communicate with
the United States. With much crackling and redialling
I did, however, manage to establish that Marvin
Lockhart was not expected to return to any of his
three establishments in Florida. Each housekeeper
told much the same story. Firm instructions had
been given not to start preparing for his return
until after Christmas; this meant that there was no
chance of his coming home for at least another three
months. Apparently it was unthinkable for Lockhart
to arrive without notice. According to a lady with a
deep voice in Sarasota, Mr Lockhart insisted on a
warm, welcoming house when he came home.

'That sure as hell isn't the case just now, ma'am.
Why, the whole place is hidden in dustcovers, the
drapes are all closed, and the rooms are in total
darkness. The sweet Jesus would have found his
manger in the inn more comfortable than what we
have here at this time.'

I replaced the receiver, the southern drawl still
echoing in my ears.

'It doesn't look as though he plans to return to
Florida,' I said to Pat.

My companion adjusted the collar of her boilersuit.

'What now?' she asked in a cheery voice, which was accompanied by a wide grin.

'I think we'll head for Malvern,' I said. 'It shouldn't take us more than half an hour to drive there. According to the map, the best way is through Tewkesbury, crossing the river Severn at Upton.'

The Royal Signals and Radar Establishment, Malvern, comprises a cluster of anonymous modern buildings nestling against the eastern lee of the hills. I entered the tallest of these buildings, some three or four storeys high, accompanied by a security guard. Taking the lift to the third floor, I was shown into a small waiting room. Below me and stretching fifty miles into the distance lay parts of the three counties of Worcestershire, Gloucestershire, and Warwickshire. Far in the distance, beyond the tuft of Bredon Hill, I could just make out the faint contours of the Cotswolds.

When he came into the room, Dr Philip Masters seemed to be in a state of some agitation.

'Was it really necessary for us to meet in the office like this, Lady Hildreth, and at such short notice?' His little body bobbed from one foot to the other as he talked.

'I intend to be very discreet,' I said. 'No one other than yourself and the director knows that I am here.'

'I can guess what you have come for,' he said. There was a rather unattractive whine to his voice.

'I am making some enquiries about the very sad death of your lover,' I said.

'A bit late, aren't you?'

He sat down beside me on a cheap modern sofa. His eyes looked tired behind his thick glasses. He passed a hand wearily through the curls of his hair.

'As I suspected, you know about me and Guy Simmonds.' His voice was flat and resigned. 'We tried so very hard to retain the privacy of our relationship. The boss knew about it, of course, and so, evidently, did you people from security. I just hope that wasn't the poor boy's undoing.'

This was the opening I needed. It enabled me to ask the central question without any further delay. 'Does that imply that you believe the security services were in some way involved with his death?'

He looked at me nervously. 'God only knows, Lady Hildreth. All I can tell you is that he wasn't the first lover I have had who has apparently killed himself. Before I came here I worked at a research station near Bournemouth. The man I knew there was said to have slashed his wrists in his bath.'

'Said to have?'

'At the coroner's inquest the only witness was someone from the police. For some reason he wasn't even from the local force. I have never been able to discover what he was meant to be doing at the scene of the accident. It hasn't been for want of trying, I can tell you.' There was a harsh edge to his voice now. 'I even tried to contact the relevant government minister. I got nowhere, of course, beyond a brush-off from an assistant private secretary. I sometimes wonder whether we really are working for freedom and democracy in this country.'

I studied him carefully to try to make out just how serious he was being. He was certainly upset; whether he was a potential traitor or, for that matter, a potential killer was less certain. It was very hard to pick out the detail of his eyes behind the thick glasses. I did wonder again about the possible implications of a homosexual network within Britain's military research establishments.

When I returned to the car, Pat Huntington's spirits continued to be exceptionally high, quite different from her mood earlier in the day.

'It's all go,' she exclaimed as she turned on the car ignition. 'The message indicator on the car phone is requesting that you call the office asap; it could be important.'

I punched the appropriate code and was immediately put through by the operator to Miss Fry MBE, the chief's assistant (she was never called his secretary).

'The chief would like you back,' Miss Fry said, with the frugal use of words for which she was renowned throughout the service.

'When?' I asked, trying to match her crispness.

'It's probably a bit late this evening. Eight o'clock tomorrow morning will do.'

'In that case I'll drive up tonight. Do you know what it's about?'

'He needs some help with the Star Wars Deaths file,' she said.

'That seems to have become the flavour of the week.'

There was a click as she disconnected herself. Miss Fry did not appreciate anything that to her sounded like flippancy, especially if it was in response to instructions she was issuing on behalf of her boss.

I turned to Pat. 'I think we'd better get a bit of a move on. Do you mind if we have supper in your house?' (This was the sentinel post from which she maintained an almost continuous watch over my cottage on the opposite side of the street.) 'I'd prefer not to make a mess of my kitchen if I've got to

64

leave for London tonight. I'll bring over the smoked salmon and the pheasant.'

'Delighted,' she said, with her good humour still fully restored. 'There's part of an engine lying on the kitchen table. I've been looking at it for that nice Mr Bird in the village. I think I'd better move it if you're coming over. It won't take me a jiffy.' I have yet to discover how at her age she managed to carry engine parts about her house.

By the time I had had a bath, thrown two dresses into a hanging bag, and rejoined her across the road, her kitchen was in functional order. That is to say, space had been cleared at one end of a large table in the middle of the room. Tools and oil cans had been piled, if not exactly out of sight, at least out of the way in the dark recesses of a large inglenook fireplace. Two place settings had been laid at the far end of the table. I sat myself at one of them on Pat's right. I was struck, as I had been so often before, by the contrast between her way of living and the beauty of her possessions. The plate in front of me was exquisitely decorated in deep blue and gold and the wineglass was of the finest Irish crystal. The cutlery was pure silver.

It was highly unlikely that she would have purchased any of this herself. It would all undoubtedly have been handed down from one aristocratic Huntington generation to another. It was the same with her lovely, mainly mahogany, antique furniture, strategically positioned throughout her three-bedroomed house. Pat seemed to treat the treasures around her not with any particular sense of pride but rather as part of the natural order of things. She didn't abuse them, but neither did she cherish them. They were simply part of her being.

'This wine is really very good, Pat,' I said. 'What is it?'

'I really have no idea. I found it in the cellar. It was a bit cobwebby when I brought it out.'

I could just make out the label on the claret bottle sitting on the shelf behind her. The name of the château was Guinot and the date looked like 1948.

'I may be away for some time,' I said. 'I have a feeling that Mr Lockhart is going to take some pinning down. Keep the usual watch out for strangers snooping around my house, especially anyone with an Irish accent. I don't suppose the IRA has completely forgiven me for busting up that operation of theirs last year.'

'On one condition.'

I raised my eyebrows in some surprise that she felt it necessary to bargain about a task she had performed many times before.

'That you keep your promise to try to get me on the next major trip.'

'Done,' I said, relieved.

# 8

I pressed the cassette into position and the sounds of Mozart's Piano Concerto Number 9 in F Major began to reverberate around the car. It was dark outside and there was little traffic on the road. I felt more at ease than I had for many weeks. I had thought I was in love with Simon Carey. After a year apart from him, I was not so sure. I could feel myself becoming immersed again in my job and the sensation was not entirely unsatisfactory. It was indeed the story of my recent life: the tension between the demands of my career and the lingering thoughts of remarriage. From time to time I even fantasized about having children. But now in my thirties, this possibility was becoming remote.

I wondered when I would be able to see Simon again properly. We needed to sort out our relationship one way or another.

After passing through Stow-on-the-Wold, I branched left for Burford. I looked at the clock on the dashboard: five minutes to ten. I released the tape and switched on the radio just in time to pick up the weather forecast. A cold front coming in from the Atlantic was evidently about to bring an end to the late-summer heatwave.

At ten o'clock the chimes of Big Ben announced the news. The first item caught my attention immediately.

Details, the announcer said, were just coming in of an aeroplane that had exploded while parked on the ground at the military airbase of Brize Norton. The aircraft did not apparently belong to the Royal Air Force, though it did seem that it was a warplane, probably belonging to an Allied country. As yet there were no reports of any casualties, but the reporter promised to provide further information if it became available before the end of the bulletin.

I switched off the radio. It was unlikely that there would be many foreign military aircraft parked at Brize Norton. Unlike RAF Northolt, it was not used regularly by visiting foreign dignitaries. The USAF had its own bases from which to make transport movements. It was possible that the aeroplane had been owned by a European NATO country. It was equally likely that it had belonged to Marvin Lockhart.

I decided that I had better try to find out its ownership for myself. The information could be useful for the next day's briefing with the chief.

As it happened, I was ideally positioned for a visit to RAF Brize Norton. The airfield was three miles southeast of Burford on the main A40 road to London. It would take me no more than fifteen minutes to be there. I pressed down my foot on the accelerator. Burford was almost deserted as I made the steep climb up its main street to the roundabout on the London road. As I approached the turn off to Brize Norton, I could see the airfield lights blazing far away to my right.

I turned on to the approach road and was immediately faced by two Royal Air Force Land Rovers placed at right angles to my path. An RAF regiment sergeant dressed in full-combat gear waved me to a halt. From somewhere above us a bright floodlight played over the scene.

As he approached my car, the airman adjusted the automatic weapon slung over his shoulder.

'Please get out of your car, madam,' he commanded through the window. I climbed out of the Mercedes and stood beside the boot.

'Are you heading for Brize Norton?' His question was strangely hesitant and apparently unpractised.

'Yes please.'

'What is your business there?'

'I have come to investigate the aircraft explosion.'

His eyes, which had been shifting about awkwardly past me, now focused themselves directly on where I was standing. I saw he was sweating under his steel helmet and I began to feel rather sorry for him. I doubted whether anyone would have thought of warning him that one of the first people he would have to stop when he set up his roadblock would be a fair-haired, slim, youngish woman claiming to be an accident investigator. I thought he was going to say, 'What's a pretty girl like you doing out at a time like this?'

Instead, the poor man asked, 'Why?'

'Because it's my job, Sergeant.'

The initiative was back with him.

'Do you have any papers?'

'Of course. I have an identity card in my bag on the front seat of my car.'

'I'd like to see it, please.'

The office pass card is not a particularly impressive

document. It does, however, have my photograph printed underneath the words, 'On Her Majesty's Official Duties.' And this proved good enough for the sergeant.

He began visibly to relax.

'You have an appointment?' he asked reasonably.

'No,' I replied. 'By chance I happened to be in the vicinity when the explosion was announced. I have some reason to believe it may be connected with a security matter we are working on.'

This had the effect of reawakening his suspicions.

'I'll have one of my men inspect your car,' he said. 'Then we'll escort you to the duty officer.'

When I arrived at the barrier to the airfield, I must have looked very important, preceded as I was by an RAF police Land Rover flashing a circular light on its roof. Certainly the armed guard at the barrier gave me a smart salute as I swept past him. Inside the guardroom I was shown into an office with a bare table and two simple chairs. A pretty WRAF corporal came in to ask whether I would like a cup of tea. This I politely declined. Then she told me I would have to wait until the duty officer came off the phone.

As she left, she closed the door firmly behind her. By an instinctive reaction, I crossed the room and turned the handle. The door was unlocked. I sat down on one of the hard chairs to wait.

When he arrived, Squadron Leader Paget turned out to be about ten years younger than I. He removed his hat and blushed attractively as he entered. Like his sergeant, he seemed embarrassed by my presence.

'Mind if I ask a few questions?' He spoke in a flat tone, rather like an air traffic controller. The strands of his fair hair were rather longer than I would have thought permissible in Her Majesty's forces.

'To cut things short,' I interjected, 'as I'm sure you're incredibly busy at the moment, why don't I simply give you a telephone number which you can ring to check up on me.'

'Fine,' he said, staring wide-eyed at me. 'Did I hear that your name is Lady Hildreth?' The emphasis was on 'Lady'.

'That's right.'

'And you're with the security services.'

I nodded.

I thought he was about to let out a loud whistle.

'When you've checked up on me, I'd like to ask you a few questions about the aeroplane that was blown up. I imagine it's a complete write-off?'

'Let's have that number,' he said, noticeably avoiding answering my question.

He returned about ten minutes later and sat down beside me.

'Your people didn't exactly make it easy for me. It was only when I said that I planned to lock you up for the night that they started to play ball. Anyway, I've now cleared it all up the line. The station commander says I can talk to you, so how can I help?'

Squadron Leader Paget may have been young, but he appeared to be competent. I was beginning to like him.

'I want to know whether the aircraft which was destroyed had an American owner,' I asked.

'That's easy,' he replied. 'Yes. What next?' He too seemed to be warming to our conversation.

'Civilian?'

'Also affirmative.'

'Do you have any other foreign-owned aircraft on the premises at present?'

'Some American Air Force general has stored a small

five-seater jet with us. I can't think why. They've got all the room in the world at Fairford and Upper Hayford at the moment.'

'Nothing other than that?'

'No.'

'Nothing that could be called a warplane?'

'Definitely not.'

'What about the aircraft that was destroyed? Do you know anything about it?'

He shook his head. 'Not much, I'm afraid. Other than that the RAF were looking at it for possible low-level ground-attack purposes. I think the trials were due to start in a few days' time. If you ask me, it looked too heavy to be of much use to us. Would you like to see its remains?'

'Might as well while I'm here,' I said, 'though as a matter of fact you've told me all I probably need to know.'

He smiled and stood up.

'I'll go and find you a good driver,' he said.

When Squadron Leader Paget returned, he was accompanied by a burly airman beside whom he looked quite small, though he must have been almost six feet.

He said, 'I have asked Corporal Mitchell to look after you until you leave the station.'

As I rose to leave, he saluted and looked straight into my eyes. There was a smile on his lips as he said, 'Good-bye, ma'am.'

The wreckage when I reached it was a twisted contortion of molten and steaming steel at which a ring of firemen was still directing a battery of hoses.

I wondered whether Marvin Lockhart would already have been informed of the total write-off of the latest sample of his creative work.

# 9

The chief stood with his back to a large fireplace. As I entered his office, his gaze remained fixed on the carpet in front of him. Immaculately dressed in a dark pinstripe suit, he seemed the very epitome of the old establishment. As always, I found it impossible to imagine him dressed up as an Arab, let alone eating the hindquarters of a rat.

One of the several qualities demanded by the Special Air Service (of which he had been an early member) was a high degree of acting ability. The chief certainly had that, to such a highly tuned level, in fact, that it was quite impossible to pick out what was real in him.

No one in the office, for instance, seemed to know anything about his friends or his relations or where he socialized or even where he lived. It was possible that Miss Fry knew something about his life outside; if she did, her knowledge was totally impenetrable.

Even his features had a certain chameleonlike quality about them: his graying hair swept back over his narrow head; his lean, slightly stooped chest; and his porcelain-textured, finely chiselled face. All, I suppose, might have belonged to a bank manager. It was not until you looked into his eyes that you began to feel the rather frightening aura of power about the man. Set deep into his face under the shadow of surprisingly prominent eyebrows, his eyes were forever changing, like the sea. But unlike the sea, they always maintained the initiative. They were never passive or merely reactive to shifts in mood and light. Sometimes boyish, even impish, sometimes fearsomely persuasive and yet at other times coldly dispassionate, they were always masters of themselves. The chief was never angry or happy; to have been either would have meant that he was not in total control of his emotions.

As I came into the middle of the room, he suddenly looked up and seemed surprised to see me.

'Ah, Jane,' he said in his slow, cultured voice (even this was capable of infinite variation). 'Good of you to drop in so early. I hope I haven't put you out in any way. I gather you've been in the country. The weather must have been very pleasant down there.'

'It certainly was, sir,' I replied rather lamely, hoping that he would come to the point soon. It was unlikely that he would have ordered me in to discuss the vagaries of the British weather.

'I gather you were at Brize Norton last night,' he said.

'That's right. Pure chance. I've put a report on tape. Do you want me to give you the gist of it now?'

He motioned me vaguely in the direction of two sofas that faced each other in front of the fireplace. He himself moved across to a large desk in the far corner of the room.

'No, that can wait,' he said. 'I'll read your report in due course. We can't put the wretched machine together again, at least not for the time being, so we might as well get on with something else.'

He came back across the room carrying a red plastic ring folder.

'I believe you have seen this before,' he said.

Typed on a label on the cover were the words *Star War Deaths*.

'Yes,' I replied, 'but only briefly, a year or so ago now.'

'Take another look at it,' he said, handing the file to me.

He sat himself in the sofa opposite, pulling his long legs to the edge of the seat. I opened the folder and began to read its contents. They were in general much as I remembered them. There were twenty-two sub-divisions, each one giving the name, circumstances of death, and nature of the classified work undertaken by an assortment of military and civilian scientists who had died unexpectedly between 1982 and 1988.

Much of the information, especially about the known causes of death, was public knowledge and had, indeed, appeared in the national newspapers. What we had apparently managed to keep secret was the highly sensitive nature of the work being undertaken by these men at the time of their deaths. We had also, it seemed, been unwilling to volunteer details at the coroners' courts of any character 'deficiencies' that might have made them vulnerable to blackmail. Sexual deviances, for instance, were listed in the notes, but not in the accompanying press reports. I doubted if this was due to any overdeveloped sensitivity on the part of the editors of the newspapers concerned. At any rate, the public was unaware that a squadron leader attached to the Ministry of Defence experimental station at Boscombe Down in Wiltshire, who was found dead in his house with a plastic bag around his head, had an interest in dressing up in ladies' underwear. Nor was it public knowledge that a nuclear scientist from Harwell who drove his car at forty miles an hour with his neck tethered to a tree was a member of an international paedophile ring; nor that a systems analyst from a well-known electronics company, who raced his car over a cliff in Scotland, was a transvestite. Nor that Dr Mike Sherwood (suicide, Shrivenham) had had copious boyfriends, including a contract mess waiter named Alastair King. Strangely, Ken Glover, Philip Masters's lover at the Bournemouth research station, was not listed as a homosexual.

'I don't see anything very new here, Chief,' I said after I had quickly flipped through the pages. 'Though, from a conversation I had with Marvin Lockhart's butler, it looks as though at least one of the facts can be corroborated.'

His response was to switch to an apparently different subject.

'You were going to tell me about Sir Anthony Dean, Jane.'

'He was at Marvin Lockhart's party the other night.'

'What sort of a mood was he in?'

'Anxious, I would say.'

'Anxious? That's not like Anthony.'

'First of all, he was shocked that Marvin Lockhart knew about the Star Wars Deaths file.'

'So he should have been.' Only in later days did I discover the full significance of this comment, which the Chief made coldly and seemingly spontaneously.

'What's more,' I continued, 'he appeared to have formed the view that we would have a much better idea of what Marvin Lockhart was about if we went back to this folder.' I pointed to the red file beside me on the sofa.

The chief stared for a moment toward the window. His gaze seemed to drift over the rooftops in the direction of St James's Park. When he spoke again, it was so quietly that it was hard to hear him.

'Was that all Anthony said about the Star Wars Deaths file?' he asked.

'No, there was one other thing. He claimed to have found new sources of information which he said were relevant. He offered to use these to help us reassess the file, on condition that we let him have a copy.'

'Ah.' The chief seemed to have found what he was looking for. 'I'm not surprised.'

'Are you going to oblige Sir Anthony?'

'Certainly not. We don't make a habit of circulating this sort of document around Whitehall.'

'Have you any idea what he wants it for?'

'I have a thought, but at the moment it's only a guess. I'm going to ask you to find a way to confirm it. I imagine it was left between you and Sir Anthony that you would get back to him when you had had a word with me?'

'Yes, that's how it was left.'

'I want you to do just that. Go and see him, preferably at his home. I believe he lives somewhere near you in the Cotswolds, Lower Slaughter I seem to remember. String him along a bit. Nose around and try to find what possible ulterior motive he might have for wishing to have a copy of this file for himself.'

'You want me to spy on one of the most senior and respected officials in government?' My concern at this prospect was, I thought, more than reasonable.

'I want you to have a chat with him in his own home.'

I wondered what the outside world, or even the chief's political masters (admittedly there was still some doubt as to who exactly they were) would make of this apparent rivalry between two departments, each of which was supposed to be central to protecting the nation's security interests.

Seemingly quite impervious to my reservations, and as if to ram home the importance he attached to this matter, the chief added, 'While you are in the area, I think you should visit the next of kin of the two murdered scientists, a mother and a wife, I believe. They both live somewhere near Anthony Dean. I would call on them first. You might pick up something that will help you with the Dean interview.'

The friendly visit to a very senior colleague had already been regraded to the status of an 'interview'. Normally in our business the term was used to describe a meeting with someone under suspicion of engaging in activities of which we disapproved.

When I returned to my office two floors below, I sat and thought for a while about the significance of the discussion that had just taken place. It seemed to be a measure of the chief's priorities in this case that the deaths of the two scientists had hardly been mentioned, and then only in passing. This was despite the fact that he persisted in calling them 'murders'. Nor had we discussed in any depth at all the current disappearance of Marvin Lockhart. What seemed really to have captured his interest was the involvement of Sir Anthony Dean.

# 10

Landsdown Castle is a nineteenth-century architectural indulgence. The turrets and ramparts that line its roof are purely decorative and have never served any military purpose. As with so many Victorian buildings, it faces north, away from the sun. Its impressiveness lies in its austerity. It is situated to the east of the main road between Bath and Stroud, close to the village of Badminton. About ten years previously the castle had been converted into a number of independent flats, to which a visitor has access through a common front door.

This was the building that I approached along a half-mile long drive-way. I parked my car at the front and entered by pushing at a heavy, somewhat dilapidated, oak door. Inside a dark panelled hall a sign indicated the direction of the various individual flats. I followed the arrow against the name 'Leatherhead.' This and two subsequent signs led me down a short gloomy corridor and up a wide flight of wooden stairs, which creaked at every step.

At the top of the stairs I pressed a bell outside a door on which there was a brass figure 5.

The lady who opened the door was both petite and pretty.

'Mrs Leatherhead?' I asked.

'Yes.'

'I'm Jane Hildreth.'

She led me inside. Her greying hair was cut short and carefully brushed to give a forelock at the front of her forehead. In the middle of a small lobby, she turned around to face me. She stood erect, with her neat bosom pressing against a crisp cream silk shirt. This was tucked into a well-fitting apple green skirt. We were about the same height. This made it easy for me to see that her clever make-up disguised the deep lines of her forehead and softened the ridges of her cheekbones.

'At least you didn't suggest coming tomorrow.' She spoke with quiet dignity, if a little nervously. 'That would have clashed with the funeral.'

'Are you completely on your own?' I asked, with some concern.

'There is no one I want to see just now.'

'Will someone help you tomorrow at the funeral?'

'I'll be all right.'

I was not so sure about this. I could sense the suppressed tension under what I suspected was a deceptively calm exterior.

She turned around again and led me into the sitting room. Two orange-and-cream-striped sofas were placed opposite each other, divided by a glass coffee table. Their erectness and symmetry seemed to suggest that they were not meant for sitting on. Mrs Leatherhead herself sat down primly on an upright chair with its back to a large bay window. I took a similar one by her side.

The atmosphere should have been totally oppressive. In fact, it was strangely peaceful and soothing. This, I decided afterward, was partly due to the rather sweet personality of Mrs Leatherhead. The reason lay also in the quite remarkable collection of pictures that covered the walls. These were all painted in oils in the most exciting and pleasing splashes of colour: hot Mediterranean seascapes, multi-coloured gardens with children in party dresses playing amongst bushes and vineyards, a complex of brightly painted deck chairs against an empty blue sky. Their common, easy style indicated that they were all by one artist.

'What lovely pictures,' I said. 'Who painted them?'

'I did.'

This trim, middle-aged lady clearly had several dimensions to her character. She stared directly at me for a moment, her hands clasped demurely in her lap.

'This is going to be very difficult, I'm afraid,' I said. 'Do please stop me if I'm becoming too pushy.'

'Lady Hildreth, I know I broke down on the phone when you rang yesterday to fix this meeting, and I may well do so again today. But please remember that I am every bit as keen as you are to talk this matter out.'

Thus encouraged, I asked, 'Did your husband have a history of problems with his heart?'

'No he did not. And furthermore, I don't think he died of a heart attack, though I know that's what they're saying.'

'You seem very certain about that?'

'Nothing is certain,' she replied, 'and I am the first to grant you that I am not medically qualified. I also know that Tom was in rather poor physical shape in the last few months. He was given to fainting fits, the most recent of which was serious, as you know. But all this was very recent. Until the threats began a

81

few months ago, he was, as far as I know, in excellent health.'

'Threats?'

Tears were beginning to well up in her large pale blue eyes. I knew I would have to be very gentle with her.

'People constantly rang in recent days, sometimes late at night, to remind him of the suicides.'

I must have looked puzzled.

'I'm sure you are aware,' she said, 'that over the past ten years or so, many government scientists are said to have committed suicide. Several of them worked at the Royal Military College of Science where, as you know, Tom was.'

'Yes,' I said, 'I do know about those deaths.'

'The work he was doing made him very vulnerable. You people in the security services really should have given him more protection. Tom used to get very upset about it. He felt no one cared. It would seem he was right.'

'Are you saying that he reported in these telephone calls, but that no one took any notice?'

'No, I'm not saying that. He never felt there was quite enough to go on. He was frightened of making a fool of himself, I suppose.'

'So, as far as you know, no one ever identified themselves as the source of the threat or, for instance, arranged to meet him?'

'As far as I know, that is correct.'

'What about foreign governments, Mrs Leatherhead? Did your husband ever mention being approached by a foreign power?'

At this question her guard finally broke down. Tears began to stream down her face. She stamped her foot and began to raise her voice. I realized by the end of our meeting that this was as much out of anger as of grief.

'Foreign governments? What have they to do with it, Lady Hildreth? The one we have got here will probably do.'

'Are you suggesting, Mrs Leatherhead, that the British government may have had something to do with your husband's death?'

'What I am saying is that more than twenty British government scientists have died recently before their natural time. The one factor they had in common was that they were all engaged in work the revelation of the details of which would have been an embarrassment to the British authorities. I am also saying that my husband did not die of a heart attack, whatever the coroner may come up with. Finally, I am reminding you that he died within a few hours of another government scientist who was cooperating with my husband on a project whose future it suits the authorities to keep shrouded in mystery.'

I had the feeling that, despite her anger, she had been choosing these last words very carefully. Her voice had quietened and she had spoken slowly and with an unnaturally clipped diction. I have no medical competence, but I sensed she was suffering from suppressed hysteria.

## 11

The road from Landsdown Castle to Upper Moseley runs northwards through the town of Cheltenham. As I struggled with the one-way system around the elegant Regency terraces, I searched for a sign for Winchcombe and Broadway. Upper Moseley was apparently situated somewhere between the two. I was still unsettled by my meeting with Mrs Leatherhead. I found it almost impossible to reconcile the daintiness and the innocence of her appearance with the astonishing and uncompromising nature of the allegations she had made.

Upper Moseley when I reached it was no more than a collection of Cotswold cottages nestling at the foot of a steep hill. The Court was easily identifiable as by far the largest house in the village. Its short drive was bordered to its right by the churchyard. The house itself looked as though it had been built in Tudor times. It stretched out along the edge of the lake, in the middle of which an island supported a mass of ducks and geese. On the far side, a small boy was rowing a rather battered looking boat.

I turned and parked the Mercedes to face down the drive and stepped out on to the gravel.

The lady who greeted me at the door had dark eyes

and black hair swept back from her face. It was not hard to make out from whom Guy Simmonds had inherited his looks.

'Lady Hildreth? Please come in.' Her accent was mid-European. 'As I told you I would be on the phone, I am glad to see you.'

She led me across a marbled hall to a large living room overlooking the lake. By contrast to the room in which I had sat with Mrs Leatherhead, this one was cluttered with ornate mahogany and walnut furniture. The several tables were covered with knick-knacks and piles of papers. The effect was not so much of being untidy as of having been well used.

'Can I fetch you anything?' Mrs Simmonds asked. 'Coffee, perhaps?'

'No thank you. I really mustn't disturb you any more than is necessary.'

'Well then, please won't you sit down?' These little courtesies had been absent at Landsdown Castle, largely, I suspected, because Mrs Leatherhead had been too shy or too nervous to offer them.

'This is my second tragedy in a year,' Mrs Simmonds began. 'I lost my husband ten months ago. Now I just have my two daughters, but they are both abroad. They are coming home for the funeral, of course. They have large families of their own, so they cannot be away for too long.'

I was struck by her serenity and wondered, as I had with Mrs Leatherhead, how well founded it was.

Her skin, in sharp contrast to her hair, was white, almost translucent, and totally without lines. She wore no make-up. Her dress was simple, a white polo-necked sweater and a long flowing black skirt. When she walked, she swayed elegantly, like a model. I assumed that she was from one of the Baltic States:

85

but she could have been from Poland or Germany. As she sat down in a gilt upright chair, she stretched forward and chose a cigarette from a silver box. She lit it with a large onyx lighter, which she picked out from amongst a group of snuffboxes and miniature photograph frames.

As she exhaled, rings of smoke chased each other toward the ceiling.

'I have known the good times and now I have the bad ones,' she said. 'Over my life I have grown to be philosophical about both.'

She paused as if waiting for some response from me. I decided to let her continue unprompted.

'So you see, I am not bitter. Life on the whole could have been much worse for me. It certainly started pretty awfully just before the war. But I married a kind, rich man, who had both the means and the desire to look after me. I was not quite so good to him, I'm afraid, but as my old mother used to say, "Never confess." Lady Hildreth, you may think I am rambling and it is kind of you to listen so far without interruption. The truth is, you need to know a little about me and, more important perhaps, about my state of mind, to be able to make a judgment about what I am going to tell you about the death of my son Guy. Such an international name, Guy, we chose it for that reason. He was a very clever man, my son. They say he could have gone to the very top of the government service. And now, phut.' She drew a line under her throat with the index finger of her right hand.

'I met him a few days ago,' I said. 'He was a very attractive man.'

'I know you met him,' she said. 'Like most women, you were no doubt deceived. My son did not make

86

love to women. He was a homosexual, but I am sure a reluctant one.'

'Reluctant? Surely it was his choice. There are no pressures on a man one way or the other these days.'

She shrugged. 'Who knows what makes us as we are – especially, Lady Hildreth, what makes men as they are? In my son's case, he was brought up with women. They were all around him, playing with him, spoiling him, seducing his mind. It was men who were for him the forbidden fruit. It was they who posed the challenge for him. He was made as he was made.'

She turned directly toward me. There was a disturbing new anger in her eyes.

'I am sure the security services knew about his weakness,' she said, 'and I believe they are using this knowledge to invent a web of lies about the circumstances of his death.'

'I understood it was agreed that he had committed suicide by breathing in carbon monoxide in his garage?'

'If that were true, why are the police not allowing me to see the photographs they took of his body?'

I remembered what Alastair King had said about the death of his friend Mike Sherwood. 'Perhaps they believe they would be too upsetting for you.'

'That's what they are saying. But they are also spreading rumour and innuendo. Our local policeman apparently told someone in the village pub yesterday that Guy had been found almost naked except for a few pieces of female underwear. The story went that he killed himself, not with carbon monoxide but with an overdose of chloroform soaked into a pair of ladies' panties.'

'If there is any truth in it, one can understand why they would want to protect you,' I said weakly.

Her eyes remained unblinking as she said, 'It's not true. Please understand the whole thing is a distraction. Not one person I have been able to talk to about this matter actually saw the body. Because of Guy's weakness, they believe they can fabricate these myths, so that the real cause of his death can be disguised.'

'But Mrs Simmonds, it is to prevent that kind of thing that we have coroners' courts.'

'I have a feeling, on the basis of what has happened to other British government scientists, that sometimes the interests of national security are allowed to influence coroners against being too scrupulous about their conclusions. Now perhaps you understand why I was so pleased when I received your telephone call.' There was a new intensity to her voice. 'You must help me to find out how my son was killed. I do not believe he did it himself.'

# 12

The civil servant rose from his chair and wandered over to the French windows. He stared out over the lawn, patched with brown by the hot summer sun. He seemed to be focusing his attention on a late-flowering herbaceous border stretched out beneath an old red brick wall.

'We've even managed to grow some edible figs this year,' he said. 'That's how hot it's been.'

Sir Anthony Dean turned around to face me, his pudgy Pooh Bear face perspiring in the afternoon heat.

'I expect they told you that we always take our holidays at home these days. That's why you've come here to see me, I imagine. Now that the children have grown up, it's not too hard work for my wife. As a matter of fact, we eat out most nights. There are some quite good pubs around here. So long as you pick and choose a bit, you can eat quite reasonably for not very much money: trout and steak and that sort of thing. My wife spends most of her time in the garden. I prefer to read these days.'

I was content to let him pursue this monologue for the time being. I had yet to find precisely the right opportunity to raise the matters that had brought me to his Old Rectory home.

I heard him say, 'I've just been reading rather a good book on the history of communism. It's got a beginning, a middle, and an end now. Communism, I mean. The absurdity of Marxism Leninism is, and always was, that it's based on the notion that there are answers to life's more interesting questions. The Americans believe the same thing from the opposite end of the spectrum. It's all very noble, but surely we should have learnt by now that however hard we try to analyse them, however clever we may be, the really interesting questions always remain that: really interesting questions. Where does the sky end? Is fairness better than excitement? Is excitement better than boredom? Is art related to either? And so on and so on. Most of these questions we first raised at our mothers' knees. If we're sensible, we know that we'll still be asking them on our deathbed. The right answers will vary from moment to moment. No-one, therefore, is right forever.'

From beyond the herbaceous border there came the disjointed chimes of church bells. I looked at my watch: five twenty-five.

'Strange time for a church service,' I said.

'Bell-ringing practice,' he replied. 'Every Wednesday.'

I decided the moment had come to engage with him.

'As you advised, the department has started to take a close look at Mr Lockhart's affairs,' I said.

'Not before time,' he replied. 'If you had been a bit more on your toes you might at least have saved his aeroplane from being blown up.'

'Any idea who might have been behind that, Sir Anthony?'

'We can all make our guesses, my dear Jane. But let's take things one by one, shall we? Did they let you have another look at the Star Wars Deaths file?'

'As a matter of fact they did.'

He sat down and lifted the lid off a silver cigarette box on a small round walnut table beside him.

'Did you find anything interesting?' He must have known that he had failed to disguise the urgency in his voice and no doubt regretted this.

'Sir Anthony, I wonder if I could start this conversation at a rather different point.' Without waiting for his response, I continued, 'I have been asked to find out a little more about why you wish to have a copy of the file.'

'Is that why you've come to see me?' The level of his voice had risen noticeably.

'It's just that the director general would like to know what use you will have for it before deciding whether or not it would be proper to release it to you. As you know, he is answerable directly to the Prime Minister on matters such as this.'

'That's something that'll have to be changed one day and not a moment too soon in my view. Not only is it dangerous to allow you people so much power, it's also thoroughly inefficient, as the nation continues to learn to its cost.'

He paused for a moment, then he erupted, suddenly manifesting the frustrations he had obviously been suppressing.

'Good God, Lady Hildreth, what cheek! What use would I make of the file? Has anyone in your world, which I fear is a smaller one than you may sometimes care to imagine, has anyone stopped to consider that it's my department which shoulders the responsibility for all those people who died? That every single one of them was either directly or indirectly under my command?' His voice, which had risen almost to a shout, faltered for a moment. I waited to see whether he was finished. It was just as well, because he soon picked up the thread again. 'Do you realize that over the years it's been I who have personally drafted literally hundreds of letters with stalling answers for ministers to send to Members of Parliament who have flooded us with questions about the so-called Star Wars deaths on behalf of their worried constituents? My ministers have even had to answer questions across the floor of the House. And you ask why I want to see the files which provide the full personal details as recorded by your agents. It's outrageous.'

His point was reasonable enough, though I sensed a certain synthetic quality about this outburst. Perhaps over the years I have become too used to senior civil servants adopting tactical positions in which they did not necessarily believe.

'Surely you have your own files on the deaths,' I suggested.

'Not with all the dirty stuff in it.' His response was a little too quick, somehow overprepared.

'You must keep a pretty good check on the personal habits of those of your research staff who are working on classified subjects. You do, after all, have your own security people.'

'It's not *my* staff I'm concerned about; it's *yours*.' At this point his tone seemed to change. It became more conciliatory. It was as if he had returned to the bargaining table having temporarily removed himself to an anteroom in a calculated tantrum.

'I'll be quite frank with you,' he said. 'I want to look at the fingerprints on these personal reports. I want to know more about the people who wrote them. I have to tell you that I believe there is someone on your team, perhaps more than one person, who has far too much access to our affairs than is good for him or, more importantly, good for us.' He added, apparently as an afterthought, 'We all have skeletons in our cupboards. I'd rather keep ours in the family, that's all.'

I watched him for a moment in silence, while he drew on his cigarette. He appeared to be staring at the sandals on his feet. The casualness of his footwear seemed somehow to symbolize the imminence of his retirement. In his thirty-odd years of service, I supposed he had escaped from any personal involvement in public scandal. I was beginning to wonder how much longer this record would last.

I decided to try to move the conversation on to a different level.

'How well do you know Marvin Lockhart?' I asked.

He seemed at first not to have heard my question. Then he stirred himself and turned to face me.

'Not very well, as a matter of fact. Why do you ask?'

'I had a feeling at his party the other night that you were quite chummy with him.'

'Chummy is hardly appropriate.'

'You dislike him?'

He didn't reply immediately. It was as if he were poised at the exit of an aircraft with his parachute on his back, making the decision whether or not to jump. For a moment the silence was broken only by the ticking of a brass carriage clock on the mantelpiece. Suddenly he sat upright. The choice seemed to have been made.

'You might as well know,' he said. 'You would be bound to find out anyway. We shared a mistress.'

'You and Marvin?'

He nodded. I paused, allowing the full significance of this to form in my mind.

Then I asked, 'Anyone I would know?'

'I doubt it. She's only been living around here for a few months. Our friendship is all very recent.'

'Has she known Marvin for about the same time?'

He took a handkerchief from the pocket of his trousers and wiped his forehead.

'I haven't a clue,' he said, 'except that Marvin introduced me to her. She used to be married to some Norwegian businessman who seems to have been a swine: too much money. She's American. When the divorce came through, she was left pretty well off. I understand she had to fight for it, mind you. She's only in her thirties. Seems to go for older men.' He smiled weakly.

'What does she look like?'

'I think most people would say she's pretty. Slim, red haired, with all the right trappings.'

'And you love her?'

He looked straight at me. 'I'm probably too old for love,' he said. 'Let's just say that I'm obsessed by her, as no doubt many other men would be who had thought they had reached the point where they no longer had the power to attract a pretty woman.'

'And you think all this goes for Marvin as well?'

'I think Marvin sleeps with her, if that's what you mean. I doubt whether he's quite so besotted by her as I am. He seems to be more dispassionate about these things, more sophisticated you might say. You must remember that until earlier this year I was a happily married man of almost forty years' standing.'

'And you're still married?' I had wanted to ask him before about the noticeable absence of his wife.

He rubbed his eyes wearily with his right hand.

'Yes,' he said, 'I'm still married. My wife's staying for a few days with her sister in Bath.'

'And this lady?' I asked. 'May I know her name?'

'What the hell for?' His response was loaded with renewed suspicion.

'I suppose she might help us to track down Marvin Lockhart.'

'Very unlikely,' he said slowly.

'How can you be so certain?'

His voice cracked. He seemed to be on the verge of tears. 'She's disappeared with him.'

# 13

'Anthony's mistress has red hair?'

'That's what he said,' I confirmed.

The chief savoured this information for a moment, then he said, 'And he shared her with Marvin Lockhart. That makes him not quite kosher from a security point of view. No wonder he wants to know who edits the damned Star Wars Deaths file. The same person could be keeping tabs on him. The shared mistress could, of course, explain how Marvin knows about the existence of the file, that is if Anthony was daft enough to tell the girl he was worried about the dossiers we keep on the personal lives of his staff.'

'It looks as though you were right not to hand the file over to him,' I said.

The chief's reaction to this was rather unexpected. All thought of the Star Wars Deaths file seemed for a moment to depart from his mind.

'We must be careful not to kick Anthony when he's down,' he said slowly. 'I can't afford to have too many enemies on the Permanent Secretaries' Committee these days. This department is not too popular around Whitehall just now. I'm afraid we've dropped too many catches over recent years, not least when we failed to get over the proper signals about the Iraqi invasion of Kuwait. Of course, we can always point to the minutes we have sent to the Foreign and Commonwealth Office warning of all sorts of disasters, but that's not quite the same thing as rubbing their noses in a firm alert. The pressures on us to be treated like any other department with full accounting to Parliament are becoming enormous. We must try not to make an implacable enemy out of Anthony Dean.'

He paused and shook his head. I had never seen him so subdued before.

'People like me,' he said, 'will find the new setup hard to get used to, though in the long run it may be no bad thing.' With this he seemed to relax. His lips stretched into a thin smile. 'Come back the Russians, I say. They were so much more convenient as enemies than this Middle Eastern riffraff. The Arabs are too remote. They don't put quite the same fear of God into the hearts of our political masters. Until, that is, one of them gets his paws on a nuclear bomb and threatens to lob it at Piccadilly Circus. As it happens, that may not be too far off now. Talking of which, Marvin Lockhart did not have Anthony's little Miss Redhead with him yesterday.'

The chief's change of subject was so fast that it took me off guard.

'Marvin Lockhart?' I exclaimed. 'Have you found him?'

'I suppose that's one way of describing it,' he replied, rather unhelpfully. 'But, as I say, not with a girl with red hair. Yesterday's companion had hair which was jet black.'

'Am I permitted to know where he is, Chief?'

'I'll give you one guess.'

'With all this talk of Arabia, I would say Iraq.'

'Not bad, not bad at all. The answer is Libya. One of our people saw him getting off a plane in Tripoli last night. His dark-haired female companion came off with him.'

'Any pictures?'

'Sadly, no.'

The rapidity of Marvin Lockhart's change in girl-friends was beginning to interest me. I decided to try out on the chief one of the theories I was developing.

'You don't think it's possible that all these women Marvin takes around with him could be one and the same person?' I asked.

'Maybe,' he said without commitment and then seemed deliberately to change the subject. 'It's not surprising that the Libyans should be in the market again for aeroplanes. From their point of view the timing is just about right. It makes sense for them to begin to make a move while Iraq's fortunes are low following the Gulf War. There are now opportunities for them to capture the leadership of the Arab radicals. In their minds this will mean building up their armed forces, especially their Air Force.'

I asked the obvious follow-up question: 'Do we have any idea whether Lockhart went to Libya out of choice?'

'Not a clue, I'm afraid. Our man naturally tried to make an assessment as to whether he had any sort of an escort, but it was impossible to tell with certainty one way or the other. It's on the cards, of course, that his lady companion was a minder.'

'Do you want me to go and get him out?' I asked. If nothing else, I saw the promised supportive role in this for Pat Huntington.

'Possibly one day, but not yet,' was the languid and enigmatic reply. 'I'm more interested for the time being in his girlfriends.'

I couldn't be certain that I was following the chief's train of thought precisely, but I had to admit to a growing surprise myself at what I was learning about Marvin's relationship with women. It was not so much the variety of his affairs as their apparent casualness that I found unexpected. I had judged him to be a man of greater depth. I wondered, in particular, how all this tied up with what the butler, Alastair King, had told me about the presence at Giddlington Manor of Lucille Fraser.

As if sensing my thoughts, the chief suddenly asked, 'How much do you know about Lockhart's sex life?'

'About as much as you learn when you meet someone casually on holiday.'

'Ah yes. You bumped into him last year when you were in Florida with your boyfriend.' I was probably being oversensitive, but I detected a note of disapproval in the way this was stated. He continued in much the same tone. 'Surely you must have found out something about his personal life?'

'Remember I only met him two or three times in pretty artificial circumstances. At that time he seemed to have a steady girlfriend called Lucille Fraser.'

'Quite.'

Now he sounded rather condescending. I suddenly felt the need to defend myself.

'Chief, I wasn't investigating him. I was having a holiday. What I saw was a rich playboy with an obsession with military aeroplanes and an apparent interest in one rather glamorous woman. He probably has all sorts of twists to his libido that escaped my notice.'

The chief completely ignored the implied protest.

'This Lucille Fraser, do you think she is important to him?'

'I thought she was last summer. But, as I say, I really have no means of assessing the accuracy of this impression. You know she's been with him over here?'

The chief chose to ignore this. Instead, he got up in silence and walked over to a side table. Apparently deep in thought, he poured coffee from a china pot into two cups.

Then, as if suddenly remembering my presence, he called over his shoulder, 'I forget whether you take milk?'

'Yes please.'

He returned with the cups and placed one beside me. When he spoke again, the tone of his voice was firm and decisive.

'I'd like a double-check on Ms Fraser,' he said. 'It could be important.'

'You've known about her all along?'

He paused and seemed to consider the question for a moment; then he said, 'Only since Mr Lockhart became interesting.'

'You want me to find her?' I was becoming rather impatient to know what it was precisely that he did require of me.

'I think we can do better than that,' I heard him say. He was speaking fast now, issuing firm instructions, the purpose of which would no doubt have been thought out several hours earlier.

'What I want you to do is to re-create last year's holiday. Get hold of your boyfriend – Simon, isn't it

– and suggest he meets you for a few days' relaxation in Florida. He's bound to be due for some leave.'

The last point would already have been checked. I wondered what Simon would make of the chief's latest bright idea. A year was a long time to have been away from each other.

'And the department's objective?' I asked.

'Florida is not a bad place to start looking for Lucille Fraser,' he said.

'We know that she has gone back there?'

'No, not for certain.' He stared at the toes of his highly polished shoes. I had a feeling he was keeping something from me. He added a little awkwardly, 'Your presence there with Simon will enable you to ask questions which will come perfectly naturally, without arousing suspicions.'

'What is it exactly that we want from her?' I asked.

He shrugged. 'Two murders have been committed. Ms Fraser's boyfriend was sufficiently concerned for the safety of the victims that he called you in to take an interest. Now he's slipped out of the country without telling anybody. She might know why, that's all.'

'You still seem sure that Simmonds and Leatherhead were murdered.'

'Perhaps I should use the word in italics,' he conceded.

I thought for a moment about bringing the chief into my full confidence, sharing with him my real worries about what he had proposed. These, as he might even have guessed, had nothing to do with Lucille Fraser.

My anxieties about my relationship with Simon Carey were real. Wouldn't it be better, if only from the point of view of my job, to allow the affair with him to die a natural death? Why revive it in this way when the embers were beginning to cool? And yet, was this not the first proper romance I had had since my marriage broke down? Despite several other affairs, wasn't this the first time I had actually considered throwing up my job and remarrying and even having children? Would it not be wise to discuss all this with the chief? Should I not treat him as a sort of surrogate father? I wondered for a moment how much practice he had had in real fatherhood. He might be able to help me to make some firm decisions about Simon. I had, after all, no one else in the world to confide in, at least, no other man. I wanted to cross the room and sit beside him. I wanted him to hold my hand, not as a lover but as a friend. How would he respond? Would he recoil in shock? Would he fire me on the spot? Or would his fingers close on mine in a comforting squeeze?

I looked over at him. His thin pale face was half turned away from me. There was no expression in his eyes. This was not the right moment. It was impossible to reveal my inner tensions to him, not now. There probably never would be a right moment. I felt so close to him and yet so far away. He was my boss: the great master spy, cold, ruthless, impregnable. He must have known about my uncertainties. It was probably why he was sending me away with Simon: to sort myself out. It would have been good to talk things through with him, woman to man. How neutral was he? I represented a large investment for the service and the service was the chief's whole life. Or was it?

That night I telephoned Simon Carey at Government House in Hong Kong.

'How is it with you?' I asked.

'Bloody awful. The Chinese here don't trust a word

we say anymore. I can't say I totally blame them. But we're going to have a hell of a job keeping the lid on things until 1997. It can't come quickly enough as far as I'm concerned. I just hope to God the Reds don't do anything silly in the meantime. We may still need their help to keep the peace. Another Tiananman Square and that option goes out of the window with all the others.'

'Fancy taking a bit of leave next week?' I asked.

There was a pause. Then he said, 'As a matter of fact, I would. It happens to be as good a time as any and I haven't had a break at all for nine months.' Then a new note of hesitation entered his voice. 'If I come back to London, how do I know that you'll be around?'

'I won't.'

'Well, what's the bloody point of my taking leave?' He sounded very tired; it was time to stop teasing him.

'I wasn't going to suggest London,' I said reassuringly. 'I wondered whether you might consider a return trip to Florida. I've got some work to finish there.'

'So have we.'

'What does that mean?' I asked.

'Work it out for yourself, love.'

'You will be coming?'

'I'll meet you next Tuesday at Miami Airport,' he said.

# 14

I replaced the receiver carefully on its stand. The chief's hunch, if that's what it had been, had been correct. Lucille had returned to Florida. 'We're meeting her at La Mere on the mainland at six-thirty,' I called out to the balcony.

A cheerful voice replied, 'Why can't Americans eat at a civilized hour like the rest of the world?'

I laughed. 'Probably because they get hungrier earlier. Possibly they work harder than the rest of us. Anyway, I don't call sitting down to dinner at eleven o'clock at night civilized.'

The louvered doors to the balcony were open wide enough for me to be able to see the elegant contours of Simon's naked body stretched out full length on a chaise longue. We had rented the penthouse apartment so that it was possible to sunbathe nude without being seen. In point of fact, except when we had made the odd sortie into the outside world to eat or to swim, we hadn't worn much clothing for two days.

I picked up two cans of Coca-Cola and pushed the balcony door open wider with my right foot. Far below, a puce water mattress floated alone on the flat surface of a swimming pool. Beyond, in the middle distance, was a tangle of palm trees, which seemed to fall over each other on to a blindingly white beach. Further away still, green and azure with heat, lay the waters of the Gulf of Mexico.

'Don't get too close to the railings. You can be seen,' Simon warned.

I recoiled to the inner part of the balcony and lay down on my back beside him. Above me a great fleet of billowing clouds commanded the eternity of the sky. The rising humidity meant that the afternoon storm was approaching. I could feel my skin moisten with sweat at the point where my thigh touched Simon's. I glanced sideways at him. His eyes were closed. There was a little gap between his lips. I leant over and ran a finger down the side of his lovely nose toward his half-open mouth. I wondered whether I would feel this comfortable with him if we were married.

'I want to drive past Lucille's house on the way to the restaurant,' I said.

'Why?'

'To have a clearer idea of the life-style she takes on when Marvin isn't around.'

'Whether she has other boyfriends, you mean. We're in for a bit of peeping tomming, are we?'

'Actually, I'm more interested in what sort of a house she lives in. One of the objectives tonight is to discover just how dependent on Marvin Lockhart she really is.'

He sighed. 'In that case, we'd better leave at around five-thirty. The traffic on Midnight Pass and over the bridge seems to get pretty bad in the early evening. Everyone chooses that time to head off the beaches in search of food. She lives just over the bridge, doesn't she?'

'Yes. We can look up the exact location as we go along. There's a map in the car.'

Predictably, the storm burst upon us at three o'clock. It was a good time for making love. Then, at around four, as if by magic, the clouds suddenly vanished and the sun blazed down from an empty sky. This was the time to swim.

At five-thirty precisely, Simon turned the rented Ford coupe on to Midnight Pass. Fifteen minutes later we were crossing the bridge that joins Siesta Key to the mainland in general and to the city of Sarasota in particular.

Sarasota is about as classless a place as you will find anywhere in the world. The reason for its existence is primarily to allow people to retire comfortably but not glamorously. Even in Sarasota, however, there are social divisions, the most visible barrier between which is a road. To the west of the road live the rich and a few megarich, and to its east live the not so rich and a few poor. The road is variously known as the Tamiami Highway, and the Trail. It cuts right through the centre of Sarasota on its way between Tampa in the middle of the state and Miami in the south.

Lucille Fraser lived on the west of the Trail in a large house on a bayou. As we drove slowly past it, we saw that she possessed, in addition to the house, an oceangoing yacht moored at the end of a lawn.

'What would you say? About eight berth?' Simon mused. The house itself was a smaller version of Marvin Lockhart's Sarasota mansion, which we had visited the previous year and which was situated a mile or so further up the coast to the north. Built in southern plantation style with columns supporting a balcony over the front door, Lucille's establishment was one of the more spectacular homes in town.

We arrived at the restaurant at about six-fifteen. The cocktail bar in the reception area was already full. When we announced to the head waiter that we were in Ms Fraser's party, the effect was impressive. He led us straight to her table, which he proclaimed was always the one by the window overlooking the bay. He was sure that she would wish him to open a bottle of Champagne before her arrival.

'Ms Fraser is obviously a regular client,' I said.

'Usually twice a week, especially when Mr Lockhart is away,' he said. 'As it happens, she hasn't been in for about ten days.' He shrugged. 'Maybe she's been out of town.'

'We drove past her house on the way here,' I said. 'Quite a place. Has she lived there a long time?'

As if suddenly realizing that he had already allowed the conversation to go beyond the bounds of the decorum that went with his office, he flushed slightly and said, 'Now, if you'll excuse me, I'll go and fetch that Champagne.'

Lucille was only ten minutes late. Somehow I had expected her to be less punctual. She was wearing a low-cut orange silk dress that ended halfway down her thighs. A mink stole was wrapped around her neck and a white Pekingese was held under her right arm. Both were deposited without a word into the waiting arms of the 'maître d'. She flicked back a strand of her blond hair, which was cut shorter and more formally than when I had seen it last.

'Darling,' she said, kissing Simon on the lips with a mouth that had been painted to match her dress.

She sat herself between us. At the age of thirty-five, or thereabouts, she was ravishingly beautiful.

'Why has it been so long? I've missed you both.

We had such fun last year, didn't we?' There seemed to be a note of anxiety in the question.

'Sorry Marvin isn't here to complete the reunion,' Simon said.

I thought I detected a pause before she said, 'Ah yes, he's working so hard, poor darling. The problem, as you probably know, is that now the Russians have got themselves all screwed up, nobody's frightened of them anymore. And that's bad for selling warplanes.'

'Surely that doesn't really bother Marvin too much with all his other interests?' I ventured.

'Certainly the money doesn't bother him. It's his pride. He likes to sell the things he invents. If he doesn't, he's like a tennis star sliding down the seedings. Now then, everyone, let's order. The lobster thermidor is excellent. All the fish is good. Though, as a matter of fact, it's not the food I come for. You see, I'm in love with Rene, the head waiter. Don't you think he's gorgeous?' She winked and I made a note to look at him more carefully when he returned to our table.

'If it weren't for Marvin, I'd lay him every night of the week. One of the joys of growing older and richer is that you can begin to make your own choices about that sort of thing.'

'I imagine you hear regularly from Marvin?' I asked.

'Pretty much,' was the unhelpful reply.

When Rene returned to take our order, he still failed to make much of an impression on me. Lucille, however, looked up into his rather gnarled, balding face with evident adoration as she ordered pâté de foie gras and lobster for three. When the Champagne bottle was empty, she ordered a beautifully aromatic white wine.

'You must allow us to pay for this dinner,' Simon offered, if a little half-heartedly.

'Nonsense, darling, this is my treat. I only wish I saw you more often.' She was looking at Simon when she said this.

Despite the quality of the wines, I was drinking sparingly. This meant, as I had hoped, that Lucille's and Simon's glasses were filled rather more frequently than mine. As the evening proceeded, she became more animated. Her cheeks, which had been quite pale when she arrived, began to colour.

Just as the empty lobster shells were being cleared away, she said, 'Britain's not good territory for Marvin. He knows that.'

'Even so, it seems he is basing himself there,' I said. 'Presumably he thinks it's a good place from which to attack other markets, Europe or even Africa, perhaps?'

For the first time that evening she looked directly at me. She hesitated. I had a feeling she was making a calculated decision as to how to respond, possibly changing her mind at least once. When she spoke, her voice was much quieter than it had been.

'I don't know,' she said flatly.

Since it was not yet publicly known that Marvin had left Britain, let alone that he had emerged in Libya, this line of questioning posed as many difficulties for me as it might for her. I decided to be more direct.

'Did he tell you that I went to a party he gave?' I asked.

Her eyes, almond shaped and heavy with mascara, tightened a little.

'No,' she said, 'he did not. What did he have to say when you saw him?'

'Much the same as you have told us. That business

prospects in the United Kingdom did not look good for him.' I wondered which of us was lying the most.

'Did he tell you what he was going to do next, about Africa and all that?' she suddenly asked.

'He hinted at it.'

'Then you probably know as much as I do.'

That begged a lot of questions. I decided to gamble.

'Libya's a hard place,' I stated.

She leaned forward and said with the slow deliberation of a drunk. 'Don't I know: Libya is a very hard place.'

As we drove back across the north bridge toward Siesta Key, I put an arm around Simon's neck and twiddled his left earlobe.

'Why Libya?' he asked.

'That's where Marvin is.'

'What's he doing there?'

'I don't know exactly and if I did, I suspect I wouldn't be allowed to discuss it.'

It was a warm starlit night. The moon's beam stretched flat across the surface of the bay.

'Let's drive to that deserted strip of beach on the south of the island,' I suggested.

'Is it the lobster or the moon that's done this?' he laughed.

'I only want to swim,' I fibbed.

'We haven't brought our swimming things.'

'I know.'

'What about the stingrays?'

'We'll keep our shoes on. Don't be such a baby.'

He pulled the car on to the shoulder on the right. Then he leant over me and put his arms around me.

'I always used to think you were pretty normal,' he said. 'You certainly were when we were growing up

110

together. Now I realize how mistaken I've been all this time. In actual fact, you're stark raving mad.'

I turned to him and said, 'Remember the tennis tournaments we used to play in together when we were teenagers? Gosh, I was mad about you in those days.'

'And now?'

I thought for a moment. We were entering dangerous territory. 'Now it's all so much more serious.'

He changed the subject. 'If only you hadn't married that frightful man Hildreth.'

'He wasn't frightful when I married him, just a bit spoilt. As a matter of fact, I think I may even have been falling in love with him all over again just before he was killed. He became so vulnerable in the end.'

'He certainly took a chunk out of our love life.'

'Simon, at the time I married John Hildreth you were not showing the slightest interest in me. You were too busy being a soldier boy.'

'I want to make up for that now,' he said.

I brushed back his golden hair and pulled his face toward mine. For me our union had now become overwhelmingly a physical one.

# 15

The next evening the lights were blazing from the many windows of Marvin Lockhart's Sarasota residence. This was itself strange. Simon turned the car around in the semicircular driveway and brought it to a halt outside the front portal, facing back down the two-mile drive.

When he had turned off the ignition, I said, 'Let's both go in. It will seem more natural.'

I looked at my watch: seven-forty-five. Outside it was already dark. Because of its latitude, the light fades fast in Florida.

There was a refreshing breeze as we stepped out into the night. Somewhere to the right a dog barked excitedly. I led the way under a colonnade of white columns to a large door. Someone must have been watching us because the door opened before I had time to press the bell.

A large black lady appeared in front of us on the verandah.

'What can I do for you folks?' she asked.

'We're English friends of Mr Lockhart,' I said. 'He told us to look him up when we were passing by.' I was conscious of speaking in a medley of English and American phraseology.

She looked at me with suspicion.

I thought she was about to retreat inside and slam the door in my face. Instead she said, 'He's not here. You've just missed him. Don't ask me when he will be back. I have no idea. I don't get told nothing these days. It makes preparing for him very hard, let me tell you.'

Once back in the car we sat in silence. I had so much to think about. Simon, sensitive to my mood, didn't speak either. I wondered what odds the chief would have placed on the possibility of Marvin returning home. Perhaps he had known all along, in which case, what was I supposed to do now?

I had to take the view that the chief would have been as surprised as I was by this twist in events and that my job now was to try to do my best to track down Marvin. Clearly the next step must be to visit Lucille Fraser.

I turned to Simon. 'We'll stop for something to eat. Then I'm going to pay a visit to the beautiful Lucille.'

'You think he may have gone there?'

'It's worth a try.'

'I'll come along to give support,' he said.

'There's no need for you to get involved. You've got quite enough problems of your own in Hong Kong.'

'Leave you on your own just when things are getting interesting? You must be joking.'

'Somehow I doubt whether this will be a joke,' I said. 'Two people have died, probably as a result of their involvement with Marvin Lockhart.'

'Let's find that food,' he said.

We stopped at the first place we came to, a lonely shack on the outskirts of Sarasota. The sign on the outside said FRESH FISH AND CHIPS. Inside, the 'special' was shark with alligator: 'the greatest double on earth.'

113

'Why not?' Simon asked. 'Apparently the alligator hunting season lasts for the next two weeks. For the rest of the year it's heavily protected. They say the meat is quite good.'

'I'll have sea bass, just the same,' I said.

A large Hispanic lady with a cigarette dangling from her lips gave me a look of unconcealed disdain. I was uncertain whether this was in response to my cowardly refusal to eat her alligator or from a sense of general disapproval at having to deal with two unwanted customers. Until our arrival, her restaurant had clearly been a haven of solitude for her.

'Let's not stay for coffee,' I pleaded. 'This place gives me the creeps.'

When he had finished eating, Simon said, 'A bit tough, but I've known worse. Okay, let's go. Can you remember the way to Lucille's house?'

'Yes,' I said confidently.

We took the Trail and headed south into town.

'If either Lucille or Marvin is about,' I added, 'I intend to force a full frontal confrontation. You wait in the car. We may need to leave in a hurry. If the place is empty, I shall have to think again. I don't have any equipment with me for a break-in. Anyway, this is a foreign country and it could lead to embarrassments.'

'You have a point,' he agreed.

Despite the relative earliness of the hour, the downtown area was virtually deserted when we drove through it. At one of the main intersections, we nearly ran over a lonely drunk sitting in the middle of the road. He was almost the only evidence of human life we came across. To our right an occasional motorboat bobbed quietly at anchor on the flat black surface of the bay. On the far side we could just make out the dark outline of Siesta Key.

We turned right off the Trail and moved closer to the water.

'Are you sure you know where it is?' Simon's voice had fallen almost to a whisper.

'When we cross the next bayou it should be immediately on the right,' I replied.

Fortunately this turned out to be correct.

'There's the wall now, with the wrought-iron gates.' Simon's voice had a quiet thrill to it.

'Drive past,' I said, 'and pull up under the group of trees on the other side of the road. I think you had better keep the engine running. You will attract less attention that way.'

When the car came to a halt I said, 'I'm going to leave you here. If I'm not back within the hour, call this number.'

I handed him a piece of rough paper on which I had written down the number of the duty officer in the office in London.

'On no account follow me,' I commanded.

'I can't believe you want to do this by yourself,' he said. 'I'll feel such a wimp, sitting here twiddling my thumbs.'

I placed a finger over his mouth and opened the passenger door. The air outside was balmy, though the breeze off the ocean was stronger than it had been further inland. I undid a button of the tropical jacket I was wearing and started to walk the two hundred yards or so back to the house. There was no doubt about it, the physical part of the job was what I enjoyed most. It was a relief to be away from the office with its endless rounds of analysis and briefing meetings.

As much as possible, I kept to the shadows of the overhanging trees. At one point I had to press myself against a fence to avoid the headlights of a passing car.

When I reached the main gates to the house, they were closed. The building itself was in total darkness. I pushed down the handle on the gate. To my relief and slight surprise it was unlocked. I leant on one of the gates and slipped through the opening on to the drive.

I began to move closer to the house. It looked empty, but I wanted to be absolutely certain. After a few moments, there was no doubt in my mind that the place was deserted. There were no lights on and it was totally improbable that Lucille – unlike the rest of the inhabitants of the city – would have gone to bed this early. The fact that the gate had been left unlocked, however, meant that I had to expect her imminent return. The interesting question, of course, was whether Marvin Lockhart would be with her.

I had to assume that I had very little time in which to complete my reconnaissance. As if to confirm the temporary nature of Lucille's departure, I soon discovered that the double garage had been left open. It was empty. If she possessed two cars, they were both gone.

I decided to have a quick look around the garage. People often drop small items as they get in and out of cars. It was possible, though admittedly not very likely, that I might find some evidence of Marvin's presence: a handkerchief, visiting card, or whatever.

I moved swiftly to the far end of the garage and extracted my penlight from the top pocket of my tunic. As I did so, I heard the sound of a car approaching. It stopped on the other side of the gates and a door opened. I heard the groan of the gates as they were pushed apart. It was time to leave the garage. I moved quickly and noiselessly out on to the driveway and positioned myself around a corner of the house, out of sight of the gates.

I was only just in time. As the car moved into the drive, the garage was suddenly bathed in light. The vehicle must have triggered off an electronic switch. Once inside the garage, the car's engine was immediately turned off and the stillness returned to the night. The car door banged once more and I could hear feet moving back down the driveway. There was a loud creak as the gates were closed. Then I distinctly heard the scrape of bolts. What was more ominous was that this was followed by the much less audible, but nevertheless recognizable, click of a lock being turned.

It had now become essential that I move to a position from which I could see what was going on. About fifteen yards in front of me, across a small patch of grass, I could just make out a clump of trees with branches all the way down to the ground. By circling to the right of the grass, I judged that I could reach this protective screen while remaining outside the arc of light thrown from the garage.

Having decided to move, I crept away cautiously from the cover of the wall of the house. I could hear the steps begin to return up the drive. Halfway across the open grass patch, I trod on a dead branch of a tree. The snap of breaking wood sounded to me like the crack of a rifle. The feet on the drive paused. I stood absolutely still. Then whoever it was began to move again in the direction of the garage.

I continued, silently this time, on my way. Once safely hidden behind the conifer branches, I was at last able to turn to face toward the house. A red sports car was parked inside the garage, its top open.

I could make out the silhouette of a figure advancing slowly up the drive. Its slimness and shape suggested that it was a woman. The tightness of her dress seemed to be making it hard for her to negotiate the heavy gravel. She wobbled forward as if her knees were tied together.

As she emerged into the light, I was able to confirm that it was Lucille. She was wearing a close-fitting long white dress. A short mink jacket covered her shoulders and her ample bosom. I noticed straightaway that there was something strange about her hairstyle. One side seemed to have been cut much shorter than the other. I felt sure that this had not been the case when we had had dinner the night before last.

When she arrived at the garage, she paused for a moment. Then she reached over the side of her car into the back seat. Her dress was so tightly strained that I thought for a moment she was going to tear its seams. Her groping became more frantic. She seemed to be getting angry. She said something which I did not catch. I assumed she was swearing.

Suddenly she seemed to make contact with what she had been searching for. A look of relief came over her face.

She unbent her body and extracted what appeared to be a bundle of human hair. She held up one end in front of her face and smiled in an apparent gesture of triumph. The strands of the bundle unwound. There was no doubt about it. She was clutching a mass of long brown hair. I thought I heard her laugh. Then she must have pressed a switch because the lights went out and the whole place was plunged once more into darkness. I heard the closing of a door and then there was silence.

My next task was to rejoin Simon as soon as possible. This would not be without its difficulties, as I assumed I was now locked into the grounds.

I made my way swiftly to the gates and confirmed that these were now firmly padlocked. I looked up at the walls on either side and decided against attempting to scale them. They were bound to be connected to an intruder alarm system. I could not imagine that Lucille Fraser would live alone without the most sophisticated protective systems. The fact that she had gone out without locking the gates must have been a careless aberration.

My watch said twenty-five past ten. I had about half an hour to get back to Simon before, on my instructions, he would feel obliged to leave his position. I looked around me. In the distance beyond the empty blackness of the lawn, the moon was reflected on the waters of the bayou. It was quite clear what I should do.

My knowledge of the habits of alligators was insufficient for me to be totally certain that they did not infest the salty waters of the Florida inlets, but I had little choice other than to risk it. I crept down to the water's edge and for a moment toyed with the idea of commandeering the motor yacht which was tied to a pier. Quickly deciding on the impracticality of this, I began to remove my espadrilles. I would rather swim with these tied around my neck than have them clinging waterlogged to my feet. It was at this moment that I saw the small rowing boat.

I sensed that the road on which Simon was parked would cross the bayou a hundred yards or so to the east of where I was. As it turned out, my estimate was fairly accurate. Within ten minutes I was sitting beside him with a quarter of an hour to spare. The dinghy was floating in the path of the moon's beam toward the open sea.

Simon said, 'I started to become a bit alarmed when the sportscar turned into Lucille's drive. I could have sworn that there were two people in it when it passed me.'

'I'm going to invite Lucille over for a meal tomorrow,' I said.

Simon looked at me in astonishment.

'Are you serious?' he asked.

'Nothing more than a barbecued steak on the balcony around lunchtime.'

He fell silent. I knew that, like me, he sensed that our holiday was rapidly drawing to an end.

It was no doubt this sudden realization that our time was fast running out that made me cling tightly to his arm as we entered our apartment. The travelling clock on a small side table in the entrance hall put the time at eleven-twenty.

'I'll ring Lucille straight away,' I said. 'She won't have had time to get to sleep yet.'

Simon went on into the sitting room and switched on the television. I could sense his restlessness. I picked up the cordless telephone and took it into the kitchen. I dialled Lucille's number and waited. There was a gap of almost half a minute before someone picked up the receiver at the other end.

'Lucille?'

'Who is this?' The voice was slurred; it sounded drugged.

'It's me, Lucille, Jane Hildreth. I hope I haven't woken you up. I tried earlier, but you were out.'

'How can I help you, Jane? It's late.' Her voice became crisper and colder as presumably she began to give me her full attention.

'I wondered whether you would be able to come over here for a simple lunch on the balcony tomorrow. It would just be Simon and me. We wanted to see you again before we left and in a modest way to return your hospitality.'

'I don't think I can do that,' she said hurriedly; there was a definite note of suspicion in her voice. I knew that this could not in any way be directly connected with the events of earlier in the evening and I decided to press my case as naturally as I could.

'We may have to leave later on tomorrow. Simon has been called back rather unexpectedly to his duties in Hong Kong. It would give us so much pleasure to see you again before we go.' I hoped this was not overdoing it.

As it happened, her voice suddenly softened and she seemed to become more relaxed.

'Okay,' she said. 'It's good of you to take the trouble. I'm sure I can change my schedule for an hour or two. What time did you have in mind, Jane love?'

'Noon?'

'You've got a deal. I'll be there.'

# 16

Lucille arrived for lunch on time, wearing a straw hat with a wide brim, heavy black sunglasses and a green chiffon wrap. Against the light from the balcony this revealed underneath what must have been one of the world's briefest bikinis and a body that was tanned.

'What a simply beautiful apartment,' she said. 'So tastefully decorated and so private. Darlings, how did you find it at such short notice?'

'We saw the sign on the road and drove in,' Simon said simply.

She appeared to ignore this.

'Doesn't the ocean look gorgeous from here? I sometimes wish I lived by the beach. The problem is that the hurricanes can get you out here. When Marvin and I were choosing a house for me, we decided to go for something as near hurricane-proof as possible.'

I poured her a large glass of wine, which she drank as if it were water.

'Simon is going to get the barbecue going while I make the salad,' I said.

'And I'll watch how you do it,' she responded, holding out the already almost empty glass. I immediately refilled it for her.

'What a gorgeous man you have there,' she said, pointing in the direction of Simon's bottom as he bent over to scrutinize the barbecue coals. I remained silent. I would have to do my share of talking in a short while.

'You're two very beautiful people. Marvin and I always wanted to get to know you much better – and I mean much better.'

Her words were already slightly slurred. I decided I would have to make my move earlier than I had anticipated. I certainly had no intention of allowing her to become drunk before we had had our little chat. What became of her after that was of less interest to me.

'Simon and I went up to Marvin's place last night,' I began.

'What did you do that for? You know he's away.' Her tone had immediately become a little menacing.

'That wasn't quite what the housekeeper said.'

'What did she say, for Chrissake?'

'Her exact words were that we had just missed him.'

Lucille dropped her glass, which smashed on the floor with the sound of an explosive device.

'What the hell are you two people doing here?' she shouted.

Simon suddenly appeared at the door to the balcony.

'I imagine you've seen Marvin in the last few days,' I pressed her.

Her face reddened and her body seemed to stiffen with rage.

'Get out of my life, lady, before someone gets hurt.'

123

Her voice had suddenly gone very quiet. When she moved, she was too quick for me. Before I could bar her way, she had reached the front door. She managed to wrench back its catch and escape into the passage, slamming the door behind her. I arrived on the landing just in time to see the elevator close behind her. By sheer good fortune from her point of view, the elevator doors must have been open as she rushed out of the apartment.

All I could do was to head for the emergency staircase and down the five flights of stairs. The elevator was quite a slow one and I must have reached the indoor car park at ground level only a few seconds after she did. As I leapt off the last step, she was running about twenty yards away from me towards her red sports car, which I saw was parked at the far end of the building.

Then something happened, most of the details of which I suspect I shall be able to recall for the rest of my life.

She seemed to stumble and her head jerked forward. As it did so, her blond hair slipped down over her face and fell limp to the ground. She hesitated for a moment, presumably considering whether to try to rescue it. Sensing that I was closing the gap behind her, she ran on. When she reached her open car, she leapt into it over the side. By the time I reached her, the car was already moving.

There was a wild, intense look in her eyes as she pressed down on the accelerator and roared toward the exit.

Her head, which was glowing with perspiration, was completely bald.

I retraced my steps and picked up the lifeless blond wig. Some of the puzzles of the previous night were beginning to fit into a pattern: the long brown hair, the lopsided hairstyle.

It was time to contact my boss.

# 17

'Most of what you have told me makes some sort of sense.' The chief spoke without emotion. 'Though I have to admit Lockhart's presence in the States surprises me somewhat. Are you sure it's true? From what you have said, you didn't actually see him.'

I had locked myself in the bathroom of the apartment and was using a telephone that was fixed beside the shower. I had no means of telling where the chief was speaking from. It was two o'clock in the morning in the United Kingdom and I had asked the duty telephonist to put me through to him. It would have been impossible for me to dial him direct; his private phone numbers were classified as secret, known only to the most senior of the switchboard operators.

'There was certainly no doubt in the housekeeper's mind that Marvin Lockhart had just left his mansion here,' I said.

'She could have been lying.'

'She didn't seem to be a good enough actress for that. We caught her completely unawares. She had no time at all to prepare herself for our visit.'

'You'd be amazed at the people who make good actors,' he said and then went silent. I thought for a moment he had gone off the line.

'Chief?' I asked.

'I'm still here.'

'What do you want me to do now?'

'Come home,' he replied cheerfully. 'There's plenty to do here.'

'What about Marvin Lockhart?'

'Leave him alone. I don't think he will go very far away now.'

'And his mistress?'

'Lucille Fraser?'

'Yes.'

'Never mind about Lucille.'

This detachment struck me as a little odd.

'You don't want me to chase her up at this end?'

'No. Come home. You'll be much more use here.'

'Immediately?' I repeated.

His reply was interrupted by a crackle on the line. When I could hear him again, a conspiratorial note had crept into his voice.

'Is your boyfriend around?' he asked.

'Yes, he's watching a programme on television next door about American policy towards Hong Kong. Apparently there has just been an announcement to say that they're not going to take any more Chinese refugees.'

'I don't blame them.' Then, as an apparent afterthought, he added, 'Is everything all right between the two of you?'

Now it was my turn to pause. I genuinely did not know how to answer his question. I felt like saying, 'If you mean our love making, it's been ecstatic. I know that's a much overused word, but I can't think of a better one to describe the excitement of what we have performed together. If, on the other hand, you are asking do we love each other, the answer is that I don't know. I think we are each too busy to be in love. Perhaps in a few years' time it will be different. Yet again, perhaps it will not. Perhaps love cannot be turned on and off. It either exists or it doesn't. When it does exist, it is all-consuming. Perhaps again it is the denial of self, the opposite of self-consuming, the ultimate moment of selflessness.'

'Fine,' I said. 'We both have an awful lot on our minds at the moment.'

I felt a tear trickle down my left cheek. I was on the point of burning yet another bridge. Soon I would be forty. Only a few years ago this had seemed unimaginably old.

'He's very handsome,' the voice at the other end of the line persisted.

'I know.' I began to sob openly in a way that I had never done before in the hearing of my boss.

'It *is* time you came home,' he said. This must have been meant as an order. Its effect on me was coaxing and seductive.

When I came out of the bathroom, Simon was sitting on the sofa, facing the television set. I sat down beside him and leant against his bare chest.

'I've got to go home,' I said.

'I guessed as much.'

'How?'

'By the length of time you were in the bathroom. I assumed you were ringing London. That boss of yours is quite some competition.' I didn't join in with his strained laughter.

'What will happen to us?' I asked.

His smile had a nervous twitch to it. 'As a middle-aged soldier, I'm a great believer in letting life take its course.'

'I love you,' I said. 'In my next life I want to marry you while I'm very young.'

'As long as you don't get hitched up to that silly sod Hildreth again.'

For a moment there was a silence between us.

Then I heard him say, 'My mother is going to be very disappointed. This was the big one for her.'

I lifted my head and looked up into his eyes. They were wet with tears.

# 18

I went by cab to Sarasota Airport. We had decided to travel by separate commuter flights to Miami. Simon was due to leave for Hong Kong six hours after I was scheduled to take off for London. We had thought it better to say good-bye in the apartment.

I cried silently throughout the entire flight to Miami. As soon as we landed, I rushed to a telephone to tell him I wanted to give up everything if he would marry me. Then I changed my mind and allowed myself to be swept along with a noisy crowd of British holidaymakers through Passport Control and towards the London flight.

Once on board I wondered whether he would have been waiting for my call. What if he had wanted to reach me? Why did we ever colonize bloody Hong Kong? Perhaps if he had gone down on his knees to me as other men were supposed to do?

My flight landed at eight o'clock in the morning. Rather than go straight to the office, I decided to call first at my house in Montpelier Square. I was exhausted. The thermostatically controlled water would be hot and I wanted more than anything else in the world to have a bath. Afterwards I would present myself to the chief.

It was only when I had paid off the taxi and was safely inside my front door that I began once more to breathe freely. One day I would pledge myself to another person, but not quite yet. For the time being, the decisions about how I lived my life would be mine alone. As if to prove this, I turned up the music centre. In response, Mozart's piano concerto could be heard on all three floors as well as, I have no doubt, on the patio. I stripped off all my clothes and left them in a trail behind me as I ran naked towards the bathroom. I would pick them up later in my own time.

It was my choice also to ring the chief from a cloud of steam and Badedas aroma while I lay sponging myself in the bath.

'Good for you, taking a bath,' he said at once. I looked at the phone in horror. Did he have the power to see down telephone wires?

He chuckled. 'I can hear the water.' Then he added, 'Don't bother to come in this morning.' I was on the point of thanking him for his consideration when he went on, 'I've fixed for you to have lunch with Anthony Dean. He has been told that you will be negotiating the details of the handover of the Star Wars Deaths file.'

'Am I?'

'Not exactly. As a matter of fact, I doubt whether the conversation will ever get that far.'

'Even when Sir Anthony believes it to be at the top of the agenda?'

'It won't be. I think you'll see my point in about half an hour's time. Enjoy the rest of your bath and then stand by to receive a parcel. I'm having it delivered to your front door.'

Thirty minutes later, exactly as he had predicted, my door bell rang. Since my involvement with the

Irish desk, I have never opened my front door without first studying the caller through a peephole. This had been specially constructed so as to give a complete and magnified view of whoever it was who was standing on my doorstep. Attached to it was a miniature camera. On this occasion, it was the chief's cockney driver, Bert, whom I knew well.

'A parcel from the boss, yer ladyship,' he announced grandly.

'Come in, Bert. Do you want a cup of tea?'

'If there's one on the boil, I won't say no.'

He carried the package with great care, as if it contained a living creature.

'What's in the parcel?' I asked.

'I haven't a clue, I'm afraid. Something hush hush, I shouldn't wonder. I was told to pick it up from Supplies this morning.'

It didn't sound much like a little personal 'welcome back' gift bought by the chief's own fair hands. I wondered briefly whether there was anyone for whom he sneaked off to Aspreys in Bond Street on a Saturday morning. If there were, Bert would probably be the best person in the world to ask. He had worked for the chief for much longer than I had. Rumour had it that they had been in the army together.

'I suppose I had better open it in my study,' I said. 'Why don't you pop along to the kitchen and put the kettle on? You know where it is.'

Bert was a little fellow who walked with a limp. He hobbled off down the passage in the direction of the kitchen.

The parcel was crudely wrapped in brown paper. Pieces of tape stuck out from its corners. It looked every bit a Supplies job. Usually, though, their parcels were hard square objects containing such items as miniature two-way radio sets and tiny bugging devices. The contents of this one appeared to be very different. They felt soft and floppy.

I laid the package on the leather surface of the Victorian desk in my study. I found myself strangely reluctant to begin the process of unwrapping it, savouring its mystery. It was exactly the same thrill of the unknown that I used to experience around the tree on Christmas Day. It was not the fact of the presents but their unwrapping which had always for me been the true source of excitement. In the same way I imagine the thrill of the huntsman's chase is greater than that of the kill itself.

I walked over to the window and looked out over the square. The leaves on the trees were turning golden. The few days that I had been away had been sufficient time for summer to begin to give way to autumn.

I returned to the desk and felt around the surface of the parcel in the way I have been trained to do as a precaution against letter bombs. Then I began slowly to unpeel the two layers of wrapping. Whoever had been responsible for the despatch of the package must, I imagine, have been told that it was to be delivered to the agent by hand and by a trusted courier. Unless the contents were breakable, there would therefore have been no need for him to be too meticulous about the quality of the packaging. I began to tear at the inner layer of paper with greater urgency. It was not until it was almost all removed that I recognized what I had received. I picked it up and allowed it to uncoil, a thick mat of red human hair.

I bent down and retrieved a white card, which had fallen to the floor. On it were written in pencil and in capital letters the words, '*RING OFFICE FOR INSTRUCTIONS*'.

An hour later I ordered a taxi and asked the driver to take me to the Naval and Military Club in Piccadilly. I specified the Half Moon Street entrance, which was the one allocated to ladies. Sir Anthony Dean was waiting for me in the small entrance hall. He had aged since our last meeting. He stooped noticeably and the few hairs he had previously had on his head had disappeared. His eyes were dulled; he looked miserable.

His reaction when I came through the door could, I suppose, have been predicted. He took one look at me and gave a start. He was clearly shocked.

'You've changed the colour of your hair,' he mumbled.

'Do you like it?' I asked. 'It's a wig.'

'I must sit down,' he said. 'Will you excuse me?'

His legs seemed to give way as he fell into an armchair.

'I'll be all right in a minute. I need a drink,' he said.

'Here in the entrance hall?' I asked.

He shook his head. 'We'll go into the courtyard. Just give me a minute.'

Five minutes later we sat at a wrought-iron table in a pleasant open square at the centre of the building.

'It's nice here,' I said. He didn't seem to hear me. We sat in silence for a moment. A large gin and tonic was set down in front of him by a dumpy little waitress. I was given a Campari and soda.

Suddenly he said, 'Red hair doesn't suit you. Perhaps it's just that I'm not used to seeing you looking like this. It's too wild. You should have brushed it harder. It ought to have been cut shorter.'

'I'll remember for the future,' I said.

He gazed in the direction of a large urn filled with pink geraniums. His left hand shook as it clasped the glass in front of him. Suddenly he turned towards me. A vein protruded down his face at the side of one eye. When he spoke the growl had disappeared from his voice. It was very low pitched, quiet, almost a whisper.

'I think I know what this is all about,' he said, 'but why couldn't your boss have had it out with me direct, man to man? It's the way things are usually done in the service. Why did he have to send you in this bizarre way?'

'Perhaps he thought you would evade his questions; perhaps he took the view that you needed shock therapy. After all, when I came to see you in the Cotswolds, you were not totally frank with me, Sir Anthony. Sharing a redheaded mistress with Marvin Lockhart is one thing; sharing Lucille Fraser with him is quite another.'

Up to this moment he had been half-slumped over the wrought-iron table in front of him. Now, suddenly, he sat up, almost erect. He seemed to have become more alert.

'What do you have on Lucille,' he asked, 'besides the fact that she is bald?' There was a new slyness to his voice.

'Let's just say that she's not particularly fussy who she picks up classified information from and who she passes it on to, so long as the cheque is made out to the correct amount.'

'Is that right?' he asked innocently.

The thought was beginning to occur to me that the chief might have sent me in order to protect Dean from a more serious interview.

'I think you know much more about Ms Fraser than you are willing to let on,' I said.

# 19

'You were right, sir, about Lucille Fraser and Anthony Dean,' I said, 'but what about Marvin Lockhart? What has he been up to?'

The chief placed the tips of his fingers on his lips. It was the first time I had noticed the beauty of his hands. His fingers were long and lean and very clean.

'I suspect that the mother and the wife of the murder victims may be able to answer that,' he said.

'Mrs Leatherhead and Mrs Simmonds?'

'They have asked to see you as soon as possible.'

'Do I go?'

'Of course.'

Two hours later, Mrs Leatherhead opened the door and smiled at me sweetly. She was looking as pert and as fresh as the first time I had met her.

When we entered her drawing room, I was not entirely surprised to find Mrs Simmonds there. She was perched uncomfortably and was rather out of place on the edge of one of the sofas. She had allowed her long black hair to fall over her shoulders, and it suited her.

'We both have the same story to tell,' Mrs Leatherhead began quietly. 'So, to save you time, we thought we should see you together. Mrs Simmonds and I have been in touch with each other quite a bit since you've been away.' She paused; she seemed to be making a careful study of my appearance. Then she said, 'You must have been somewhere nice, judging by your healthy looks.'

I let this pass, and Mrs Simmonds intervened.

'Our purpose is a very serious one, Lady Hildreth. What we have to relate vindicates what Mrs Leatherhead told you about the death of her husband and what I said about the killing of my son.'

'I have come straight down from London within a few hours of returning from America to listen,' I said.

'Shall I speak for both of us?' Mrs Simmonds asked. Her companion nodded.

'Very well. The day before yesterday we each received a strange visit. It was from a man. He arrived unannounced in both cases. Normally neither of us would have let him in, but his voice sounded elderly and he said he had information about our dead loved ones. This was, you will understand, too much for either of us. We each invited him in. In Diana's case it was around eleven in the morning.'

'He was very lucky to find me in. I normally go out shopping in Bath at about that time,' the little widow chipped in from her upright position on the dining room chair she had pulled up beside Mrs Simmonds.

'In my case he arrived about four in the afternoon,' Guy Simmonds's mother continued.

'What did he look like?' I asked.

'He was tall, good looking in an ageing Clark Gable sort of way, with a clipped moustache and an American accent.'

'What did he say?' I was conscious now that my growing interest was making Mrs Simmonds's task more difficult. Quite unfairly, I was forcing her to tell her story at an unnaturally fast pace.

'He came to apologize.'

'What for?'

'For the deaths of our two men.'

'Did he confess to killing them?'

'No, but he said he could have saved them.'

'Was that all?'

'It was good enough for us, Lady Hildreth. I'm sure you understand. There is now no question of suicide or death from natural causes. Our men were murdered.' Her foreign accent had become quite pronounced.

'This man left without naming the killer? Perhaps he didn't know.'

'Oh yes, I think he knew all right. I believe his problem is that he doesn't dare tell the authorities for fear that they will want to extend the cover-up. He seems convinced that his own life is in danger now.'

'So having apologized to you, he just left?'

'Not quite. We both said we had been talking to you. This seemed to cause him some relief. He said that you would know where to find him if you wanted to pursue the matter.'

'You really think he believes these two deaths are part of some official conspiracy?' I asked.

Mrs Simmonds shrugged. 'Yes, and of course we agree with him. Are you really surprised by this? After all, there has never been any public enquiry, no official statement. Just silence; and this is meant to be a free country. I wonder sometimes whether my people will soon have greater freedom than you do here. As I am sure you know, I come from Poland.'

139

# 20

I lifted the handset of my car phone.

A familiar voice said, 'That you, Jane?'

'How have you got on, Pat?' I asked.

'I've got bits of branches in my hair and I've torn the seat of my pants on some barbed wire, but otherwise I couldn't be better. It's been a wonderful day so far.'

I smiled to myself. 'What on earth have you been up to?'

'You asked me to check out Giddlington Manor.'

'I only asked you to give them a ring to see if Marvin Lockhart was about.'

'That's what I did. I followed your orders to the letter.'

'In that case how come the ripped pants?'

'There was no answer, so I went over to look for myself.'

'Ah.'

'Very interesting.' Pat Huntington clearly felt the need to justify her initiative.

'Really?' I tried to register my disapproval by disguising my interest.

'Don't you want to know what I found out?'

'Of course.'

'Marvin's back.'

'How do you know? Did you see him?'

'Not exactly.' She chuckled.

'Come on, Pat. What happened?'

Despite our age difference of almost forty years, Pat Huntington had become one of my closest friends. Nevertheless, I was irritated by her at the moment. All I had asked her to do was to ring Giddlington Manor on an invented pretext and find out whether Marvin had been back or was expected to return in the near future. I had not anticipated that she would turn the event into some sort of paramilitary adventure. I should perhaps have known better. My concern now was that she might have frightened him away.

'What happened?' I repeated.

'Do you want all the gory details?'

'Only if they're relevant,' I sighed.

'Okay, here goes. When there was no answer on his phone, I drove over to Little Giddlington and parked the car in the village.'

'Was it the Lagonda or the Buick?'

'The Rolls actually.'

'It must have stuck out like a sore thumb. There's only one street in the whole village.'

'It won't have been there for very long.' For the first time she sounded a little peeved and I resolved not to interrupt her again, at least not until her story was complete.

'Sorry,' I said. 'Do go on, Pat.'

'There's not an awful lot more to tell,' she said. A sulky note had entered her voice. 'I made my way up to the house.'

'Along the drive?'

'No, through the woods. That's how I ripped my

clothes. When I was close enough, I used my binoculars, the ones the office gave me before they kicked me out. They're not bad, as a matter of fact.'

I recollected the binoculars had been a bit of a mistake at the time. Despite the excellence of their make and their considerable optical strength, Pat had accepted them with less than her usual grace. I had felt at the time that this was not just because they marked her departure from the service, but also because she took them as in some way a slur on her eyesight, which was still that of a top marksman. At least the present adventure had finally put them to use.

'So what did you see?' I asked.

'Cars. Several of them parked in the drive. Quite different from when we were there last time.'

'Were there any people about?'

'No.'

'So what makes you think Marvin's there?'

'If he isn't, they're giving quite a party in his absence.'

'I suppose they've probably gone by now,' I said with some resignation.

'I can assure you they haven't.'

'How do you know?'

'Because I'm speaking to you from behind a bush overlooking the entrance to the drive.'

For the first time I laughed out loud. I wondered what a stranger would make of a seventy-odd-year-old lady lying under a bush in the middle of the English countryside with her trousers torn and sporting a high-frequency radio transmitter and a pair of binoculars.

'I'm about ten minutes away from you,' I said. 'Don't shoot me as I come down the drive. I'm making straight for the house. As long as you're comfortable, perhaps you could stay where you are until I leave. Let's have dinner at Alexis's Restaurant tonight.'

'On one condition.'

'What's that?' I sighed.

'That this won't be the last time I'm asked to guard your escape route. I'm getting a taste for active service again.'

'I heard you,' I said. 'I'm looking for some more excitement myself, and I think I'm on the manhunt again.'

I pressed a button and the window beside me slid down. A warm breeze began to blow around my shoulders.

## 21

Marvin Lockhart looked old and haggard when he opened the front door to me.

'I have been expecting you,' he said simply. 'Let us talk in the study.'

I followed him across the hall to a polished mahogany door in the far right-hand corner.

His appearance, normally so immaculate, was dishevelled. The top button of a dark blue shirt was undone and the knot of his tie had slipped a few inches. His grey hair was longer than when I had last seen him and the ends of his moustache drooped over his upper lip. His eyes were red with fatigue.

He opened the door for me and we entered the room he called the study. This was more of a large drawing room, although the walls were lined with leather-bound books and in a corner to the left there was a large Victorian desk covered in papers.

Marvin waved me wearily toward a high-backed chair and he sat himself opposite me. Beside us an open fire spat menacingly on a wide stone hearth. When Marvin spoke, he did so slowly, with deliberation, apparently searching with some difficulty for the right words to introduce what he wished to say.

'I know what you want to hear,' he said, 'and I will

do my best to satisfy you. But first, I shall need to digress a little. Please be patient with me. I must tell you a little more than you know about myself. You will see the significance of this later.

'You know me as a designer of military aircraft. I guess you probably think I'm a bit cranky, but you may have some respect for my abilities in that direction. You will not be surprised to know that I too am proud of some of my work. At least two of my machines have been very good. But many people have designed aircraft before and many more will no doubt do so in the future. Even if their products will not be piloted by human beings and will be called by some other name, in essence, they will still be aircraft like mine. They will have to obey the normal laws of aerodynamics.

'But my heroes are not the designers, who are the stuff of back rooms. My heroes are the guys who work in the front rooms, or, better still, on the streets. These are the people who persuade other people to buy. They are the true artists in my gallery. If I had the time left to me, I would want to write an epic poem in praise of salesmanship.'

He lifted his gaze from where it had been fixed on the flames in the fireplace and stared directly at me. One of his eyelids drooped a little. In the space of a few weeks he had become an old man.

'Maybe it's because I've never been very good at it,' he said, 'marketing, I mean. I am sure you know, Jane, that I have never sold a single one of my aeroplanes. That isn't very good, is it?'

His once-militarily-straight shoulders were slumped forward.

'One of the greatest salesmen I ever met', he continued, 'was a five-foot-tall waiter in a run-down coffee shop off Forty-second Street in New York City. He used to warm up his customers by telling them that he was half Italian and half Spanish. He then announced that he was also proud to work for the establishment which made the best cheesecake in the western world. He couldn't speak for the east because he had never been there. "Well, we don't actually make it," he would say, "they make it in Pennsylvania. You know where Pennsylvania is? I just told you, it's where they make the best cheese-cake in the western world." Without giving you the opportunity to respond, he'd shout into the service elevator, "Hey, Luigi, I need one more order of that delicious cheesecake." I saw him go through this routine many times. Never once did I spot anyone who had sufficient courage to decline the cheesecake when with a triumphant flourish the sticky mess was placed before him.

'I never found out his name, but he was a true artist. I once asked him whether he could do the same thing for aeroplanes and he said, "Hey fellow, it's getting late. It's time you went home to your wife and kids." That was the last time I saw him. When I returned, the place had been closed for development.'

I decided it was time to interrupt him. 'Where is all this leading, Marvin? I must warn you I am interested in the deaths of two British scientists.'

'So you should be,' he replied.

'There are strong reasons for believing they were murdered,' I persisted.

He removed a green silk handkerchief from the top pocket of his tweed jacket and dabbed his forehead with it.

'They *were* murdered,' he said.

146

I remained silent, determined not to reveal my growing interest.

'It's all very simple, Jane. I knew at an early stage that your government was stringing me along.'

'Lucille Fraser?'

He nodded.

'She ran between you and Anthony Dean?'

'You could put it like that.'

'And that is how you came to know about the Star Wars deaths?'

'Yes. Lucille is a very wonderful person. I really do not know what I would do without her – unbelievably loyal.'

'Loyal?' I asked. 'Don't you mean greedy?'

The light was poor but I thought I saw his cheeks colour. If so, I suppose this could have been caused by the heat of the fire.

'I don't pay Lucille for information,' he said, with a new stiffness, 'though I concede that others may. She is certainly an accomplished actress. I think you will find that her affection for me is real enough, though God knows I've given her a hard time over the years.'

Suddenly he struggled up from his chair and leaned over the fireplace. Lifting an iron poker, he began to prod a smouldering log.

When he resumed his seat, he said, 'Did you know that she even shaved her head so that she would be able to wear the wigs more easily?' His voice had become low and confidential.

'She worked for you for love?' I tried to hide my scepticism.

'I think so.' He paused and then added quietly, 'I'm sure of it.'

'And she slept with Sir Anthony for money?'

'Perhaps.'

'And that is how Sir Anthony came to tell her of his worries about the contents of the Star Wars files?'

'It wouldn't be the first time that a man has been indiscreet with his mistress. Before you decide to arrest him for it, you will no doubt wish to judge exactly what lay behind Anthony Dean's anxieties.'

'Guilt,' I suggested.

Marvin looked straight at me. He was about to say something. Instead he shrugged and sat back in his chair. For a moment we faced each other in silence. It was very frustrating. I felt I was close to learning the truth about Sir Anthony Dean's real interest in the Star Wars file. I was certainly beginning to suspect that this American had it in his gift to be of considerable help in this respect. He seemed to be reading my thoughts.

Suddenly, he leaned forward and said, 'When you came to my party, I had only recently learned from Lucille about the fate of the twenty-two scientists.'

'Dean's version or what the files say?'

'Surely the whole point is that Anthony doesn't know exactly what exists in the files. That's what frightens him.'

'Lucille told you that as well?'

'Of course. That's what his hang-ups are all about. He cannot be certain how much you people know about the causes of the deaths.'

'Why should that bother him, Marvin, unless he was directly involved?'

For a moment he coiled back in the shape of a foetus into the recesses of his chair. Then he sat forward again, more alert than before.

'That is for you to decide,' he said. 'All I can tell you is that when I learned that most of the deaths

148

had occurred in the establishments where Simmonds and Leatherhead worked, I was scared as hell.'

'I am surprised,' I said.

'Why?'

'Why should you worry for the safety of Simmonds and Leatherhead merely because in the past there had been certain suicides in their places of work?'

Marvin threw his head back and stared straight at the ceiling.

'Perhaps you do not share my view of the complexity of Sir Anthony Dean's position,' he suggested. 'You see, I have reason to believe that what he told Lucille was done not just out of stupidity. There had to be a clear purpose behind it. He meant to tell her about the Star Wars file. He wanted her to relay the information to me.'

'It would interest me to know how much you encouraged Ms Fraser in all of this,' I said.

He closed his eyes for a moment.

When he opened them again, he said, 'I think that is rather a personal matter, don't you? I didn't get a charge out of her relationship with Dean, if that's what you mean.'

'Let me rephrase the question,' I said. 'Why would it be Sir Anthony Dean who would want to convey information to you? Surely the boot was on the other foot? Surely it was you who, through Lucille, was pumping him?'

When he looked at me this time, his eyes were very tired.

'It's a long story,' he said wearily. 'Are you ready for it? I will have to start way back with my belief that Anthony Dean has been working for at least one foreign power. Why don't I explain over dinner? You will stay for dinner, Jane? My butler, Alastair King, will be disappointed if you do not.'

149

## 22

'Would your ladyship like to wash before we serve dinner?'

I hardly recognized the voice addressing me from the far corner of the room. It was precise and professional, very different from the tormented tones of the last time that I had heard it. On the previous occasion, Alastair King had been in disarray and apparently in a state of some shock. Now he stood by the door to the dining room, erect and dutiful. His black butler's tails were still a little loose fitting for his thin torso, but his hair was perfectly combed back and his thick black-rimmed glasses were set squarely on his sharp nose.

The office had managed to track down some useful background material on Alastair King.

'Ah, Mr King, I have been meaning to contact you,' I said. 'One thing you failed to tell me when we last met was that you had worked for some time for Sir Anthony Dean. I understand you were with him for several contract periods.'

The butler removed his glasses. For a moment he concentrated on polishing them with a napkin that he held in his right hand. When he spoke again, the Birmingham edge to his accent was more pronounced. It gave a slight whine to his voice.

'As I explained,' he said, glancing at Marvin, 'I have worked for many different people in my time. Sir Anthony Dean was certainly one of them. I did not understand when we happened to meet, Lady Hildreth, that you were looking for a catalogue of my former employers.'

'No doubt I shall be told in due course what this is all about,' Marvin interjected. 'In the meantime, let's go in to eat.'

Mr King gave a curt bow and opened a pair of large double doors. We entered a long, panelled room, at the far end of which was a small minstrels' gallery. Down the centre was a table, which I assumed could seat two dozen people. On this occasion, only two place settings had been laid. As we sat down, Marvin at the end of the table and I to his right, someone dimmed the lights and the table began to warm to the flickering glow of three tall white candles placed in front of us.

Mr King unfurled my napkin and laid it on my lap. I watched him carefully as he withdrew the top from a decanter and began to pour sherry into the smallest of the six glasses laid out before me. Presumably he would have guessed that I had discovered his prison record. I would, however, have been very interested to know what would have been his reaction to learning that so far I had completely failed to find any history of violence on his files. What was clearly not in dispute was his skill at butlering. He moved about the room with stealthy efficiency. After the sherry came an excellent white wine, heavy with bouquet. This was accompanied by rich slices of marinated salmon. When he had finished serving this course, Mr King temporarily withdrew.

As soon as he was out of sight, Marvin said, 'He's a very good butler and he has been very helpful in these difficult times. But I have to say he has started to give me the creeps. It's almost as if he is too involved in everything. He seems to get very emotional about it. Dammit, I only employed him through an agency as temporary staff on, I may say, the recommendation of Anthony Dean.'

'Let's continue our previous discussion while he's out of the room,' I suggested.

'Okay. Let me start again with the relationship between Lucille Fraser and Sir Anthony Dean.'

'Encouraged by yourself?'

'We had that out before,' he said. 'I have to admit that from my point of view there were certain benefits in it. One of them, as I have said, was that Lucille learned that the British government were not a serious prospect for my aircraft. As a matter of fact, this was not all bad news for me. For a start, it brought me some helpful appraisal work, free and for gratis.'

'Care of Simmonds and Leatherhead?'

'Exactly. But much more important, it provided me with a reference from which to negotiate with a government which really was interested in my product.'

'Libya?'

He looked at me intently for a moment. Then he said with growing irritation, 'It seems I may be wasting my time. You know it all already.'

'The important thing is that I hear it from you,' I answered.

'I entered into what I thought were proper commercial discussions with the Libyans. It was quite clear that they were serious in wishing to take up where Saddam Hussein had left off.'

'As leaders of the new Moslem imperialism?'

'That's one way of putting it.'

152

'And you were willing to help them?'

He picked up his glass and began to sip his wine. When he finally spoke, there was a new urgency in his voice. It seemed suddenly important to him to reassure me on one specific matter.

'You must understand,' he said, 'money had little to do with it. It was always a question of my pride in my aeroplane and the obsessive need I had to find a customer for it; someone who of his own free will had come to a decision that he needed it. I wanted to see it fly effectively, of course, but what was much more important was to have pitted myself against a buyer and to have won.'

'And once again you were let down?'

'It was not so much that. That happens the whole time in a marketing situation. The catastrophe for me was that once again, as you put it, I allowed myself to misjudge the real motives of the buyer. No good salesman can ever do that and continue to hold his head up high.'

'And the murders?'

'Please let me deal with them in sequence.'

Frustrating though it was, I had no choice but to allow him to maintain his own pace.

'It quickly transpired that the Libyans were not so much interested in buying my aeroplane as in getting their hands on my drawings.'

'That's why you returned to America to collect the plans?'

He stared at his plate, which was now empty. Then he raised his right hand and rubbed his forehead. He seemed for a moment to be at a loss as to how to continue.

Finally he said, 'At first I refused. Then the threats began.'

'The blackmail came directly from the Libyans?'

'In one sense, yes. That is to say, it was a Libyan who came to tell me that if I did not comply, one of my aircraft would be blown up.'

'Was that all?'

'By no means. For me that was much the least chilling of the threats. My aeroplanes are properly insured; they can always be rebuilt. What was much more frightening, from several points of view, was their statement that unless I followed their demands, they would start to kill some of those who were associated with the aircraft.'

'And you believed that they would carry out their threats?'

'Not immediately.'

'What changed your mind?'

'Three words: Star Wars files.'

I looked at him with renewed interest. A line of sweat trickled down his left cheek.

'How do they come into it?' I asked

'In two ways, my dear Jane. First, there was the fact that the Libyans knew of their existence. Secondly, and most significantly, the Libyans knew that I was aware of the files. You can see how this might give some credibility to their threat that in the event of my continuing to refuse to release the drawings, they would despatch Simmonds and Leatherhead with the same mystery that was attached to the other twenty-two deaths.'

I allowed the full implications of this to sink into my mind.

'You are saying that it was critical to the Libyans that you should be aware of the files in order to give some force to their blackmail?' I asked.

'I'm suggesting rather more than that,' he said.

'I'm saying that someone pretty knowledgeable at this end must have been in direct contact with Libya to provide them with the knowledge of the files in the first place. That is why I said in answer to your earlier question that it was only in one sense that the threat came directly from Libya. Someone over here was also pretty closely involved.'

'There are a number of points that still don't add up,' I pressed. 'First of all, you are implying that the Libyans eventually carried out their threats and murdered Doctors Leatherhead and Simmonds.'

He nodded. 'That is correct.'

'But the coroner's verdicts were quite clear: a heart attack in Dr Leatherhead's case and "suicide" for Dr Simmonds.'

I had my own reservations about these judgements that it was important now to find out what Marvin's were. He looked straight at me.

'Ever heard of Iraqi poison?' he asked.

'Of course. It's the slang name for thallium, the colourless rat poison.'

'Then you'll know it's almost undetectable. It has fooled pathologists in the past and no doubt will do so again in the future.'

I was rather surprised by the depth of his knowledge on this matter, but let it pass.

'And so what happened to the aircraft drawings?' I asked.

In the half-light thrown by the candles I could see that an old man's bony arm began to shake on the armrest beside him.

His voice suddenly fell into a whisper. It was hard to make out exactly what he was saying.

'For me that was the ultimate humiliation. When I saw the disastrous course events were taking, I returned to Florida and collected the plans. After I had delivered them in Tripoli, they took them away for an hour; then they returned and threw them down on the floor in front of me'.

'"We don't want these any more, Mr Lockhart," they said. "Your plane is too slow for our purposes. It is only good for conventional weapons. We want a machine that will deliver nuclear warheads. Your aircraft is not suitable for this."'

Mr King chose this moment to reemerge from the shadows in order to clear away our plates.

'Is pheasant all right for you, your ladyship?' he asked. It may have been a trick of the light, but a strange, almost triumphal look seemed to have entered his eyes.

# 23

'We have been paying good money to Lucille Fraser
for months,' the chief stated flatly. 'Total waste of
resources, of course. I only hope the Public Accounts
Committee never gets to hear about it. Dean has
simply not dropped his guard. He probably guessed
she was working for us.'

'You would expect me to be surprised and I am,'
I said. 'If Lucille was shadowing Sir Anthony the
whole time, why did you put me in to bat against
him, especially with the strange wig idea?'

The chief got up and walked toward the window.

'It would have been useful to have had a full
confession,' he said.

'And you thought I might succeed where Ms Fraser
failed?'

He didn't seem to be listening.

'Now we may never know the extent of his involvement with the Star Wars deaths.' His voice had
dropped almost to a mumble.

'And why the false trail to Florida?' I asked. 'If
Lucille Fraser was on our payroll, why was I sent to
interview her?'

He tapped his nose with his right forefinger.

'I don't trust anyone in this business,' he said, 'and

nor should you. I wanted a double check on her. Don't forget she once took a hefty present from Anthony Dean for sleeping with him. God knows what she may have collected in Tripoli, let alone from Marvin Lockhart.'

'I don't understand why, if we paid her, you couldn't use her as a witness against Dean,' I said.

He paused for a second; the hesitation was almost undetectable.

'She has told us nothing which could incriminate him,' he stated, 'nothing at all.'

I felt it was time to change the subject.

'The autopsies on Simmonds and Leatherhead showed no trace of poison, not even thallium,' I ventured.

'I know,' he replied, 'the coroner had no choice but to return verdicts of "suicide" and "natural causes" respectively.'

'Do you believe Marvin Lockhart's tale?' I asked.

'Which bits of it?'

'For instance, that they were both killed by the Libyans.'

He was now standing with his back to me, facing the window. I couldn't help noticing how perfectly tailored his suit had been to fit his straight lean shoulders.

'I think it's too convenient,' he said.

'Convenient for whom?'

'Anthony Dean, for one.'

'Marvin did implicate Sir Anthony.'

'That part of his story doesn't amount to a row of beans, all circumstantial and hearsay, very tenuous stuff.'

'What do you think he's been up to, sir?'

'Who?' I sensed that my boss had suddenly become rather distant.

'Sir Anthony Dean.'

'Encouraging our defence scientists to flog our secrets abroad, I shouldn't wonder.'

'Then bumping them off when things got too close to him?'

'Something like that.'

I couldn't help noting his sudden evasiveness. My hunch was growing firmer that the chief's heart might not be fully in the Anthony Dean chase. Perhaps there had been a deal between the two men. Sir Anthony had been left with a peaceful retirement while the skeletons in our departmental closet had remained untouched.

'So we add the Simmonds and Leatherhead deaths to the other open files?'

'The short answer is yes.'

He turned round to face me. His eyes were cold and piercing. The room seemed suddenly to have gone very quiet. By way of comfort, I tried and failed to conjure up a vision of Simon Carey, suntanned and uncomplicated.

'Never mind about Lucille,' the chief had advised on the phone to Florida. What he seemed to have said now was, 'Never mind about Sir Anthony Dean, even if he is a traitor and a mass murderer.'

The light was beginning to fade. His figure was becoming a mysterious silhouette against the window.

Who was this man? Tall, powerful, brilliant, brave, middle-aged, perverse, mercurial, cold, ruthless, detached. I did not even know his Christian name. Suddenly it had become important to me to find out much more about him. I should correct myself. It was the intensity of this feeling which was new. The feeling itself had been with me for many months. It was the reason why I had not been able to love any other man.

159